Between the Sand and the Sea

Rob Ritchie

Ritchie, Rob, 1964-

Between the Sand and the Sea / by Rob Ritchie

ISBN 978-1-55483-508-9

Editor: George Down
Cover Photo: Bella Brough
Design and Typography: Ardith Publishing

Published in 2022
Colpoy Editions
Box 1363 Wiarton ON
Canada N0H 2T0

Visit the author at:
www.robritchiemedia.com

Other novels by Rob Ritchie

Orphans of Winter

In a Company of Fiddlers

A Song With No Words

For all of the generous wordsmiths
who make the North of 45 and Word Compass Writers' Retreats
such a magical place

~

She brings no possessions with her ... no phone, no purse, no history. Likewise she offers no footprints by way of name or vocation. She is, in fact, nothing more than the sun and water upon her skin, spending her afternoons floating on the wavelets, delighting in the chance that the lake, on one of her warm and sun-filled days, might use its gentle current to drift her into the path of another.

~

Chapter One

~1~

The raging surf crashes over the breakwater, striking her waist high. Pelting rain stings her eyes and cheeks, and a relentless wind pounds against her chest. Still she struggles forward, the length of her footsteps diminishing as she pushes into the teeth of the gale. In ten strides, she will be thrown from the concrete walkway by the counter-force of a wave retreating back into the lake. Having been so focused on bracing against each incoming surge, she will fail to heed the power of the storm's recoil.

Her initial moments in the water will be spent frantically gulping for breath and flailing her limbs, vainly searching for any kind of solid purchase. Then claustrophobia will set in – the panic of being trapped between crests like jagged swarming mountains, folding in her horizon, closing off any and all points of reference.

But she will rally from this terror. She will gather herself, albeit temporarily. She will find a reserve of fortitude to synchronize her arms and legs, orient her body horizontally and roll her face skyward. In doing so, she will steal the few safe breaths necessary to scan the fading sky for anything useful ... the outline of a tree, the roof-top of one of the taller shoreline homes, even the breakwater itself from which she has just been hurled. But the storm front has swallowed the beach whole. There is no east or west, no in nor out to her merciless surroundings.

She will have no choice but to aim for where she thinks she remembers last seeing the faintest glow of light. Up and over successive towering waves, the dark ink of each undulation looming higher than the previous until finally the inertia of a coiled wall of water crashes over her, sending her spitting and sputtering anew, cartwheeling from her stomach to her side to her back. She will summon every abdominal muscle, windmilling her arms, pedalling her legs, now in the mere hope of gaining just a speck more time and space for a few more gasps. She will crane her neck one last time for a glimpse of something to mitigate the hopelessness that has returned to envelop her. But this effort too will fail. She will again somersault down the fall line of the swell, dumped back into a gorge of angry water, even as her probing toes haplessly cycle beneath her searching fruitlessly for any hint of the lake bed below.

In time – precious scraps of time – fatigue will drain her. She will spend her last few moments taking stock of her existence. Her mind will race in search of her most meaningful life markers. Achievements. Relationships. Family. 'This is my end,' she will then tell herself, just before she is greeted with one last fleeting respite.

It will come in a flash of recollection of a distant fable she once read. Something about a man hanging from a ledge by his fingertips halfway down a cliff. Atop the precipice, a tiger awaits with teeth bared. Below, a valley floor of jagged rock a thousand feet down. On the ledge in front of him grows one lone ripe berry. The dangling man reaches with his lips to snare the fruit, and chewing on its brief flesh determines it to be the most flavourful morsel he has ever had the fortune to taste. This will be her final thought as the last bit of residual light leaves her eyes. With no fight or fear left in her, she will slip below the water's surface.

~2~

Pyette Beach Up-To-Date Admin

Welcome to the Pyette Beach Up-To-Date Facebook group! Thanks for joining us!

A few guidelines to get you started. Please note that this is an information and recreation-based resource for all things Pyette! A place you can share and receive the latest sights and sounds of our wonderful vibrant beachside community.

We do strive to maintain standards through a few simple rules of conduct which go a long way towards keeping this site a safe, enjoyable and entertaining outlet for you and your fellow group members.

Firstly, please be polite and kind in your interactions. Postings should not be belligerent or aggressive in tone, nor should they be derogatory against any specific ethnic, religious, or socio-economic group. Demeaning and offensive comments or posts will not be condoned.

Secondly, while debate forums and platforms are a necessary part of life in today's world, this is not a page for political views to be aired, argued or challenged.

> *Thirdly, while the posting of information related to the business interests of Pyette Beach, (i.e. restaurants, merchants, gift shops), is encouraged, this is not a site for direct commerce. Posts advertising the direct sale or rental of merchandise, property, or services will be removed by the administrators.*
>
> *That said, it's great to have you on board! And thanks for becoming part of the Pyette Up-To-Date Community. We hope you find it an enriching environment.*

It was, to Erin Leith's way of thinking, a curious usage of the word *environment*. The would-be writer in her found it far more awkward than the literal environment of a beach – a location she had known so well and fondly as a child.

Her parents, for all their considerable affluence, had never caught anything in the way of a travel bug. So they had eschewed distant and exotic locales for holidays close to home in an annually rented cottage next to Lake Huron's shore, not more than a half-hour's drive from their home and business ... year after year, the last week of July through the first week of August.

She remembers most the feeling of the sand. More than the lake, it had been the primary attraction for her and her cousin (and occasionally her older brother ... until adolescent beach endeavours superseded). The digging, the burying, the flinging ... the building of miniature canals and motes around miniature castles that made up miniature wash-away worlds perched precariously close to the creeping wake. True, there was probably just as much time spent *in* the water, splashing, diving, sputtering ... battles over air mattresses, and the occasional cannonball launches from the shoulders of disinterested fathers and uncles. But for Erin, any memory of worth always ended with her chilled and waterlogged, racing back to shore to hug herself into a plush towel, and then, as soon as possible, dropping to the softness of the well-baked sand to pour handful after handful over her goose-bumped legs.

Absent-mindedly she scrolled through the Facebook group's postings for that day ... someone found a watch on a bench at the south end of the beach, someone had posted a picture of some peonies in front of their cottage, someone had offered video of the horizon at sunrise with the white froth of the waves rolling up onto the shore. She clicked on it and instantly she was back in time, her imagination supplying the soundtrack – the steady ebb-and-flow-rhythm that had greeted her from the front loft of the rental, every morning of those vacations. So strange that such a powerful and recallable *environment* had simply ceased to play any active role in Erin Leith's life ...

... until now.

It had begun quite innocently, with long purposeless mid-afternoon drives, first through the countryside, down county roads and concessions she had never before travelled. Some cut a straight line through endless fields of corn and hay. Others ran serpentine, nestled beneath the foliage of a forest as they twisted ribbon-like through woods – *hiding roads*, she had called them as a child – their path teasing the adventurous traveller to trust in a reason for their existence, and therefore trust in a reason for their exploration. After a week, these routes had transitioned to a game of hopping from town to town, taking in the modest charms of quiet main streets. Period buildings of red brick, spruced with freshly painted trim and adorned with contrastingly rustic accents from a pioneering past – wagon wheels, milking cans, wheelbarrows. Heritage gently honoured.

Perhaps too honoured, she had decided one day, after having driven her meandering town-and-country circuit steadily for a week or so. For at that point she could not help noting how each town and village no longer offered anything different from the last. An antique store here, a yarn shop there. Another restaurant, another café, another independent hardware store. For a day or so, she was alright with the realization, telling herself that the medicine of these impromptu excursions was not to *find* any particular place, but rather to enjoy the state of being nowhere in particular. To be in the countryside and farming hamlets, but not *of* the countryside and farming hamlets. To be as a camera lens would – there to accept whatever passed the eye. Which would have been all well and good, had she not – one afternoon later, following a series of brand new indiscriminate lefts and rights – found herself no longer in the gentle swells of farmland, but out against Lake Huron's shore. It was a destination not more than a forty-minute drive from her own front door had she taken a direct line. And yet, an *environment* she had rarely visited since her childhood.

~

Erin Leith noticed two people in particular on her first visit to the beach. The first was an older woman with orangey-brown leather tanned skin, riding on a vintage bicycle. Slight and sinewy, with long white hair that danced carefree across her face, she unapologetically sported a two-piece black swimsuit, a pair of flip-flops and nothing more. Erin watched as the woman, without any hint of concern for anyone around her, dismounted, adjusted the fabric around her crotch, and pulled a blanket, a paperback and a water bottle from the handlebar basket. She had quick darting movements and appeared impressively lithe for someone probably in her late sixties. She also seemed completely and utterly at ease with her surroundings. This was not a passing tourist. No, for this woman, the beach was home.

Erin imagined the woman owning one of the nearby cafés or boutiques – perhaps the candle shop on the lakefront road. Imagined her having run one of these establishments for decades, maybe even as an inherited business. Perhaps she was a long-standing pillar of the community, rooted in its traditions, yet free to be a windblown spirit out along this spit of sand. Like beach grass.

Perhaps she had raised a family here, too. But if so, had her children moved on and outgrown a need to be by the shore? Or were they too – like this woman seemed to be – irresistibly drawn to keep vigil next to this endless shimmering horizon? And would they in turn, once they reached their later years, finally answer the same calling of their mother and return to a lakeside sanctuary to reside vibrantly and comfortably in their own weather-beaten skin?

Leaning on the steering wheel and craning her neck a little, Erin watched the woman drop her belongings to the sand and, without breaking stride, march straight out into waist-deep water where she disappeared beneath the surface. Although she would see the woman in passing on several more occasions that summer, the two would not meet. They would, in fact, never so much as exchange a wave or passing nod. Nevertheless Erin would credit the stranger, by her mere presence that first day, with granting her the necessary permission to get out of the car and head across the road to the beach-side swimwear shop.

~

The second person of note was the complete antithesis of the woman on the bicycle – short, squat and completely overdressed for the scorching heat that had accompanied the day.

Having bypassed the overcrowded sands of the main beach, Erin had strolled the shoreline north to a sidewalk which split a few hundred metres further on. The right-hand path proceeded into the gated marina and yacht club. The left fork circled out to the town's government dock, which stretched diagonally into the lake, forming a breakwater sheltering the beach's swimming area from the full force of the lake's waves. Here she had located a series of huge flat-topped boulders packed into the seaward side of the structure, the perfect option for that part of her still in negotiations over whether she should be there in the first place. It did, after all, at least lend itself to *activity*. Because she could not – would not – abide the pastime of simply lying about inert. Could not imagine herself merely digging her heels into the heated granules, splayed out alongside the narcissistic and self-possessed who carpeted the sandy beach proper back over her shoulder. Too much folly. Too much idle awkwardness. But give her these boulders to climb and hop about on, these boulders from which she could launch into the shimmering water, dive down and drag a fingertip along the sandy bottom ... well, that was far more justifiable to any hypothetical passer-by, wasn't it? His or her hypothetical voice calling out, "Is that Erin Leith out there swimming? Good for her, getting in some exercise."

Having selected one of the larger pinkish-grey rocks, she had just nicely lowered herself waist-deep into the lake when the woman caught her eye. She too was older ... perhaps mid-seventies, perhaps more. Her hair was set in a way that reminded Erin of her own mother's weekly rinse-and-set rituals, sprayed firmly and crisply in place, impervious and impenetrable to even the stiffest of breezes. Maternal comparisons ended there, however, as the woman's crimson lipstick and over-enthusiastic rouge radiated far more grandly than the restrained tones that comprised her mother's make-up regime. Similarly her attire. She wore capri pants and a blazer, both in squint-bright white. Her V-neck underneath the blazer was pink, with an exceptionally busy floral screen print down the front. And then there were her accessories. Or accessory, to be accurate. Clutched in her hand was not a purse or tote, or beach umbrella, but a long cord affixed to a bright pink balloon bouncing kite-like in the air. *Happy Birthday* was emblazoned in large block letters on the side.

Erin offered a smile which the woman returned amplified, flashing a cigarette-yellowed grin that seemed nothing less than completely proud, as if the moment, in and of itself, was somehow a profound accomplishment. The woman held her pose for several seconds, the only movement being short quick head nods which eventually managed to coax a weak hello from Erin's lips. Then, as quickly as she had appeared, she was off, waddling her way out onto the breakwater.

Erin hoisted herself back onto her stone, letting her feet dangle in the surf a moment, then pushed off again, this time to float on her back in a gentle semicircle, all the while keeping an eye on the puzzling woman, now almost all the way out to the end of the dock. Watched as she happily ambled a rhythmic meandering path, as if she were singing along to a musical in her head. Gently, almost reverently, she uncoiled the string from around her wrist to hold it in both hands. Then with arms extended upward, she turned toward the horizon and let the balloon go, staring motionless as it drifted up and away until it was a mere speck lost against a cloudless sky.

~

"How's the water?"

Erin spun around to find two men approaching. Twenty-somethings, both in board-shorts. One in black, the other a powder blue. Flip-flops. Sunglasses. Shirtless. Both were walking bikes towards the breakwater's walkway. She wasn't sure which of them had spoken, or indeed if they had spoken to her, which mitigated her attempted response. A slight nod and – much to her own surprise – a thumbs up.

"She has the right idea," black shorts called over his shoulder to his friend, as he dropped his bike unceremoniously against the rocks. "Let's go in off these boulders." He was tall and slight, curved in his torso, giving him a look that seemed equal parts enthusiasm and awkwardness. Adventuresome, but a bit at odds with his own dimensions. Erin could relate. (*Stand your height* had been a constant unsolicited mantra to be endured from her mother and her Aunt Bernice throughout her growth-spurt years.)

"Todd, come on, she's already here," the other replied, pointing at Erin's belongings and returning a nod towards her. "There's lots of room down this way." But his friend was already in the water, having kicked off his sandals, flung the sunglasses behind him, and cannonballed just to her left.

"Sorry, we can get out of your way," the second man said with a smile that, strangely, she found more intrusive than the nearby swimmer.

"No worries," Erin said and leaned back, lifting her feet to float straight out from shore with a couple of backstrokes, trying to tune out the closer man's thrashing about by focusing on the sunny sky above – an unadulterated azure whose accompanying warmth toasted her forehead and contrasted with the cooling ripples pooling across her ribcage. For the next few moments she was lost in the task of reacquainting herself with the lake of her childhood. She arched her back and crested her hips above the surface, curled her feet beneath her, then floated upright to gaze back at the rocks on shore. Only then did she once again take stock of the newcomers' whereabouts.

The shorter tanned man, true to the letter of his words, had moved down the rocks, though he was still well within shouting distance of his friend, as they bantered about the water's temperature and depth. He, like Erin, swam a linear path out and back from the boulders, though perhaps at a subtle angle, carving a route that, while not encroaching on her swimming space, certainly did not evade it. For the next ten minutes or so they maintained their proximity – and a mutual awareness of one another. She said nothing. He only spoke overtop of her to his friend, who was now back on shore, sunning himself atop the breakwater's retaining wall. Eventually, she extended her swim further out into the lake a hundred feet or so, periodically gliding under the surface, blowing bubbles, making her body as streamline as possible, arms out in front, fingertips pointed, legs locked straight, feet and toes extended behind her. But upon her return – was it just in her imagination, or did she sense again a desire on his part to stay near, feel a deliberateness to the way his return to dry land was coinciding with hers?

"You okay?" he asked as she climbed from the water to a slippery ledge of stone and reached for a dry purchase higher up the rock.

"Yup, good," she said, decidedly stone-faced as she reached for the towel she had purchased along with the new suit, (which with a now-or-never shrug of her rounded shoulders, she had worn straight from the fitting room mirror, across to the beach). Spreading it out on top of her boulder, she sat down with her knees drawn up towards her chest. *Still your move*, she thought she heard a voice in her head say, as she glanced down to the exposed crease between hip and thigh. It had been a very long time since she had heard that voice. *Longer still since you let your thighs out in public*, the voice replied, as she yanked the towel out from under her and draped it strategically across her waist.

The shorter man pulled himself to shore three rocks down, calling over to apologize again for his friend encroaching on her swimming spot. She replied – again – that it was no problem, and straightened one leg out towards the water, hugging the other tighter as she kept her eyes on the horizon. He asked if she was vacationing. She replied no, but said nothing further, choosing instead to jump back in the water for three more out-and-backs, watching him spectate out of the corner of her eye. Only at the end of her afternoon, as she wrapped herself in the towel, picked up her sandals, and tossed her T-shirt over her shoulder, did she finally look over and say something. Not a good-bye, or have-a-nice-day, but: "Thanks for sharing the beach." This, she would still be mulling over at length on the car ride home half an hour later, still sporting her brand new swimsuit, with the car windows wide open to let the newfound summer in. *Well, look who pulled out the coy,* one of the many voices that lived inside her head piped up. *And you, what? Fifteen years older? Twenty?*

~

Had anyone she knew happened by on that first day, Erin might have instinctively begun offering an explanation for her presence there – an explanation she began cultivating for her own assurance (and her voices) that very first drive home.

There would be a fair bit of poetic detail concerning the allure of the mid-afternoon sun shimmering on the water ... how it could dance so beautifully on the spray of a Great Lake wave. There would also be descriptions of the act of swimming itself. The weightless joy of a shallow dive, followed by two or three long underwater strokes along the bottom of the lake bed before gliding up, eyes toward the polished underside of the surface. Erin Leith did, after all, fancy herself a bit of a writer. And she believed a writer – a true writer – needed the ability to describe things into a state of higher worthiness. Like the boulder she had found, for example – worn smooth from thousands and thousands of years of the lake's repetition, its contour now affording her a platform from which the water could receive her. (True, as a writer, she was a work in progress.)

They had seemed such a necessity at the time, these rationalizations. It was important for her to frame the afternoon as nothing more than a long overdue communion with a cloudless sky and a refreshing lake. Sun and solitude. A pilgrimage of sorts. A higher purpose than the masses who regularly pitched their blankets all over the sand, wallowing in the company of strangers, awash in the lingering odour of lotions and sun sprays. Young and old. Fat and thin. Bronzed and browned. The splashers and swimmers. The nappers and would-be nappers (their truth hidden behind the dark tint of designer sunglasses), the magazine skimmers, the phone surfers and text-ers, the selfie-takers. She needed to deny any degree of kinship with them whatsoever. Deny even the slightest fraction of interest in being in their midst. And as an outer membrane of truth, this sense of differentiation would get her through the rest of her drive home that first day.

But, of course, back to the water's edge the next.

~

Moments later a second figure emerges from the cloudbursts. She has traced what she believes would be the first's most likely route ... out through the waterlogged dunes, down the trail toward the marina, itself now a swiftly flowing waterway ... then out to the government dock. And though each successive thunderclap sucks a fresh scream from her lungs, she does not stop. Panic-stricken, she will aim straight into the headwind, crying out into the jaws of the storm, as she shakes the barrage of rainfall from her face, throwing the moisture from her chin, all the while her eyes boring a window through the deluge.

With no thought for her own well-being, she will jump down the supporting rocks on either side of the breakwater. On the slightly sheltered inward flank she will find no one, so she will cross to the outer ledge, even daring to step out onto the boulders now under full assault from the storm. For a moment she will be spellbound by the jagged contours of crashing surf lashing at her feet – the relentless undulation of the horizon beyond grinding and heaving the lake and sky into one. Then with another thunderclap – and another scream on her part – she will be off once more, fuelled by dread. She will lower her head and struggle toward the far end of the dock. She will continue to bridge the distance in a zigzag pattern, staggering back and forth along the breakwater's length, scanning the blackened waters in both directions. And though the howl of the gale will swallow all sound as soon as it leaves her, she will not give up screaming out the woman's name.

~3~

Erin Katherine Leith was born on March 16, 1979, in the city of Owen Sound, Ontario, the second of two children to Douglas and Marilyn Leith. The Leith family had been synonymous with the downtown furniture business that bore the family name for decades. Doug was the fourth generation to own and manage the enterprise which had been founded by his great-great-grandfather in 1903.

Like his forefathers Doug worked in the store all of his adult life, taking over the reins late in 1978, just months before the birth of his second child. He ran the business until 2008, when the pressures of big box furniture outlets popping up on the city's outskirts, and a family doctor's concern over the businessman's chronic high blood pressure, bade the Leiths draw the curtain on their century-old retail landmark. (It was a concern which proved warranted when Douglas collapsed from a heart attack while out golfing the following May)

In the intervening decades, thanks to Marilyn's steadfast devotion to her husband's charities and interests, the Leith name was also synonymous with civic philanthropy. The Leith Foundation oversaw the maintenance of three separate parks connected by a scenic walking trail – likewise a community tennis court and ball diamond. Their surname could be found etched high on the donor plaques at both the hospital and the library; as it could on the scholarship lists for a half-dozen high schools in the county. Thanks in no small part to her tireless efforts they were, if not the first family of this small midwestern Ontario city, at least in plain sight of whomever held that position above them.

All of which occasioned the need for appearances, (though Mrs. Douglas Leith would never choose to put the matter in those words). Rather, she would speak of her efforts in terms of a familial duty that she, through marriage, had proudly inherited like all the other Leith spouses who had gone before her. At its heart, this duty was an obligation to reflect their life station in deed, and dress and propriety, and for Erin's mother such obligations were beyond debate. All those who followed down the branches of the family tree, if they were not being groomed to head up the furniture cause, were expected to pursue a path of at least equal importance. And to their credit her husband's siblings had outdone themselves. Douglas had been the oldest of five sons. Next in line was Henry, who had studied law and then gone into politics, serving a stretch of consecutive terms as mayor of the city between 1968 and 1980. Cedric had studied medicine and taught obstetrics at U of T. Martin had entered the Anglican ministry, made deacon at the age of thirty and bishop of the Huron diocese by forty-five. And while James unfortunately succumbed to leukemia a month shy of his seventeenth birthday, George, the youngest, had forged a career in education, first as teacher, then principal, then Director of Education for the Wellington County School Board.

As a teenager Marilyn Cyr had worked weekends in the Leith furniture store all through high school, even picking up extra hours in and around her nursing classes at the Owen Sound General and Marine Hospital. It was there she met and began courting the store owner's son. Their first date, a movie and ice cream, fell on her eighteenth birthday. They were wed a week after she turned twenty. *Me, of all people*, as she was often heard to say in spreading the news of the pending union, the only child of Normand and Martine Cyr, both line workers at the bookbinding factory on the east side of the harbour.

~

Todd and his friend returned on Erin's fourth visit to the beach. This time they were further down the shore, with a number of friends – all slim and fit young women and men, carefree as they jumped from the rocks, cannonballing ... laughing, splashing. She watched as Todd grabbed a young tanned blond woman by the waist. She jumped, then with a playful shriek, reversed his hold and climbed up to piggyback on his shoulders.

"Looks like they're having fun."

The voice had come from directly behind. Before she could turn around, a woman appeared, climbing over Erin's stone, reaching with her foot to hop onto another just off to the left. In the process, and without introduction or apology, she placed a hand on Erin's shoulder to steady herself. Erin waited as the woman squatted down on her perch and smoothed out a small striped cover-up. She half-expected something more by way of conversation. But instead the woman shielded her eyes to pan the flashing silver horizon, north to south, then leaned back on her hands as she splashed at the lapping water with her toes. She adjusted her swimsuit – the straps, the underwire, the waistband – busily brushing undetectable granules from her stomach, inspecting herself impassively ... her outstretched legs, left then right with heel folded and toenails brightly polished in a coral, pointed out. She wore a higher-cut bottom with a bold geometric pattern trading on oranges and yellows. Higher-cut and a bit smaller too, Erin noted. A bit more ... more what? (The voice in her head was trying to pipe in with *daring*, if not a term more dubious.) Erin, however, settled on *free*.

Like Erin, she was tall. Five foot eight or nine, Erin estimated after lengthy consideration, afforded by her location slightly behind the woman. Possibly also by the fact the woman seemed completely comfortable with their proximity – as she stretched away any stress from her body, closing her eyes, tilting her chin towards the sun.

She was also prettier, Erin determined immediately – far prettier. And it was an active, athletic kind of prettier. An honest prettier. The woman's shoulders were less rounded than the curve that greeted Erin sidelong in the shower door's reflection every morning. (*I'm still trying Auntie B. ... Christ knows, I'm trying.*) Her dark hair was straight and tied off her face with a scrunchy. Her skin was a deeper complexion than Erin's – a natural golden brown, all the darker from the summer's rays, save for the woman's feet. A runner, Erin guessed. Out of doors daily with shoulders and legs exposed, but feet firmly wrapped in the sturdy confines of a pair of cross-trainers. She found herself drawn to the woman's shoulders. Wondered whether she herself could attain a similarly bronzed hue by summer's end, then instantly admonished herself for the thought. *Tanning as achievement – really*? Like an item on a to-do list. *Christ, woman, what are you doing here?* the voice demanded.

But there was also something in the woman's motion. From the safety of her vantage point, Erin observed the woman continue to flex her legs one at a time, stretch her arms behind her back, then up and over her head. There was a carefree grace to her movements. One that suddenly made Erin Leith long for the chance to go back and take a childhood's worth of dance lessons. God, why had she never tried? Why had she never pestered her parents like so many other daughters? That was, after all, she concluded on the spot, the essence of attraction, wasn't it? Beauty was not some impassive stare from a pouting-lip fashion model, no matter how many magazines and ad campaigns promised it so. Beauty was motion. Beauty was how legs (*like those?*) leapt and ran. Beauty was untamed hair blowing in the wind. More subtly, it was how a smile changed a face, how eyes could ignite in sunlight. Beauty did not sit and pose. Beauty ran, and it played and danced ... and maybe even swam.

Erin got to her feet to step around the woman and dive in. Arms stretched out, chin tucked, back straight, she slit the surface and with just a couple of powerful strokes covered twenty, then thirty feet, her chest skimming close to the sandy bottom. Gradually she glided at an angle back towards the surface, flipping onto her back once it was breached, to feel the welcome sensation of clear water tempering the hot sun.

She glanced back to shore. The woman had not followed. (*And why should she?*) Maybe not so much a swimmer, Erin surmised after several more dives to the bottom and a rigorous front crawl out alongside the breakwater ... hard pulls from the shoulder down, propelling her a hundred metres or so ... then a slower, casual side-stroke back to her rock. She was just a few feet from shore, trying to decide on some nugget of introductory small talk, when the woman jumped to her feet. Once again she brushed at her torso, her thighs and calves. She reached for her beach cover, which she held but didn't put on. "Enjoy the water," she called over her shoulder and climbed back over the rocks, out of sight.

How old would she be, a completely new voice asked. *Thirty-five maybe?* Well ... thirty at least, Erin hoped. For some reason it was important – imagining her to be at least thirty.

~4~

Sanjeev Thakore

Haven't been to the Beach in a few years, but planning on visiting with a few friends the week of the 6th through 13th. Would it be best to book motel rooms ahead of time?

Celia Andersson

You'd have been best to book last March. Everything's full up through Labour Day

Mitch Young

Afraid yer SOL buddy

Pyette Up-To-Date

Mitch Young Manners please?

Mitch Young

Same old story isn't it? As soon as these clowns are north of Toronto, they think there's nothing but vacancies and campsites, and all of us just waiting to be graced with their presence.

Pyette Up-To-Date

Mitch Young ...all part of being a tourist-industry community, I will remind you.

Sanjeev Thakore
Actually I'm coming from Fredericton, New Brunswick.

Beth Armstrong
Best option would be to find some accommodation in one of the nearby towns. You'd be a half-hour away from the beach, but at least you'd have a place to stay.

Erin tossed her phone on the passenger seat and edged out of her parking space. As soon as she was settled in traffic, she flipped on the radio just in time to hear the host of an arts-talk show introducing a brand new segment featuring a brand new pop-culture columnist. This was followed by hyper-paced promises from said columnist that in the coming days she would *deep-dive* into what was trending, and would *unpack* the many, many new and exciting developments across all social platforms. (Or words to that effect.)

For some reason the radio had become an integral component of Erin's beach-day regimen. Perhaps, at some level, listening to news, and taking in opinion pieces and editorials, lent a further sense of legitimacy to what were still – to most of her voices anyway – afternoons of nothing more than folly. But if that was in fact the case, the current program was falling short. There was something off-putting about this particular columnist's quota-free usage of the word *like,* something as well in her unmitigated penchant for up-speak. *(Up-speak is on the rise*, Erin mouthed, congratulating herself with a smile out the open window.)

As the two studio voices prattled on about a new release by some apparently seminal band whose name she did not know – then a movie from a director whose listed litany of previous works contained no familiar title – it became apparent amid the a-fore-noted *likes*, and responsive *I know, rights?* bouncing back and forth like recreational tennis, that whoever this program's intended demographic was, she was not it.

This bothered Erin. It was the same lingering feeling she sometimes encountered when she caught too much of her own detail in the bathroom mirror, or an unflattering reflection from a storefront ... even the side window of her own car. (Et tu, Kia?) Suddenly there she would be, looking far more worn and second-hand than she had been prepared for. It wasn't about any sagging imperfections, or drooping body parts. Not really. Because, the truth was, Erin found she could still take inventory of her anatomical pros and cons and feel she was doing reasonably okay. No, these moments were more a case of an unanticipated glimpse at something that suggested emptiness. The suggestion of a story-less life. Which made for a sad irony, really – that Erin Leith, the unquenchable devourer of literary fiction, too often felt unworthy of living a tale of her own. And, of course, tangled up in these unwelcome moments was the nagging fear of time. Not of time gone by, but of the days yet to come. The banal fear of *this is it*. Of realizing her future – once complete – might be just as effectively conveyed with a thousand pages of prose exhaustively describing the depth of her mediocrity, as it could with a diary filled with blank pages.

Near the conclusion of the radio interview, the host finally touched on a topic with which Erin had at least a passing interest – The Tragically Hip. It came in the form of a reminder that in just a few weeks it would be the anniversary of charismatic front man and singer Gordon Downie's last concert, which he performed, *as we all know*, while in the final throes of his battle with cancer.

There was something further – something about an upcoming podcast to honour the event. Erin didn't catch any more particulars, for mention of the band had already flung her thoughts back to when she first heard about the singer's illness. Her cousin Trevor had phoned within the hour.

"Did you hear?"

"I did."

"Shit this one hits hard, Cuz. Remember the Aud in Kitchener. When was that? '96? Christ that's so friggin' long ago. You remember that?"

Of course she remembered. She went with Trevor and his girlfriend (that week), Melanie, who spent half the night pulling on Erin's arm imploring her to escort her to the washrooms. Meanwhile Trevor, along with a couple of other impromptu best friends, had split the expense on a bag of weed from some enterprising teenager and bounced their way through the crowd to the front of the stage.

Strictly speaking, she had not been a fan. She had never found the timbre of Mr. Downie's voice particularly pleasing. Nor had she really ever been able to discern *the sheer fucking profound poetry of his lyrics* – as Trevor attested – from the drone of his own unique vocal delivery. But she had tagged along at the urging of her cousin. End of school year. His treat.

"I swear, Cuz, once you go, you'll get it. I know at a glance The Hip can come off looking like some over-glorified bar band, but I promise, there's so much more to them. Hell, my communications prof quotes them in class at least once a week ... minimum."

It was a claim she would hear more than a few times over the years whenever social conversation was steered to music and the Canadian scene. And not just from her cousin. It could be whenever she was in the presence of twenty-somethings turned thirty-somethings lamenting the state of the recording industry ... often accompanied by a diatribe on the degeneration of musical tastes amongst those dreaded millennials. It happened at barbecues, at dinner parties, the occasional staff-room debate ... and one miserable evening during a one-and-only attempt at a vacation in Florida.

"Once, with my cousin and his friends, in Kitchener," she had offered poolside when a balding snowbird had inquired if she'd ever attended a Hip concert. The question had been mostly stammered into the bottom of his fifth gin and tonic, shortly before the man – whom she would unsolicitedly learn was down from Barrie, Ontario for a real estate convention – went off at length on the band's appeal. With an ever-increasing slur, he strained to compare his beloved Tragically Hip to the sport of hockey which, apparently, Mr. Downie liked to write and sing about. "Take any Leaf home game ... although Gordie's a diehard Bruins' fan. But you know what? Doesn't matter. Take any Leaf game on any night of the week and you've got lawyers and car salesmen sitting beside farmers and auto workers, all cheering on Gord and the boys just as loud and passionate. Limos partying with pick-up trucks, that's the beauty of The Hip right there."

It was an annoying conversation at the time, and annoying in retrospect, but she had to admit that the assessment – reeking of mans-planation though it was – rang true, if for no other reason than the fact the band's music had captured the heart of two people as diverse as this blowhard and her counter-culture, all-things-organic cousin. Erin could still hear Trevor shouting *best show ever!* into the night sky at the top of his lungs as he hopped down the length of the parking lot, grabbing her by the shoulders from behind and vaulting ahead to lead the charge toward the nearest pub.

She shook the memory loose, returning to the radio voice. She was trying to listen closer. Trying to summon a greater degree of emotion for the occasion. Trying sincerely to separate the matter of Gordon Downie's artistic merits from the grating pitch of the radio host filling her car with noise.

~He put small-town Canada on the map ... from the byways of Bobcaygeon to the Saskatchewan Prairies.

"No, I believe they were always there, if you bothered to look," Erin mumbled to herself.

~And he championed all things Canadian.

"Did he? Bruins' fan, you say?" she blurted out louder and instantly felt bad for doing so. None of this was the issue. Not the columnist. Certainly not Gordon Downie – Rest in Peace. The issue was ... well, what the hell was the issue? That she couldn't conjure up requisite sympathy on demand? That the universal appeal The Hip held for seemingly everyone had managed to evade her? That she had no personal experience of *championing* anything for herself? That apart from these recent lakeside sojourns, lately ... no, not lately ... actually for quite some time now ... she had felt only ... only what? Anything at all?

~

Even when presented briefly as mere skeletal information, family history occasioned a certain level of suffocation for Erin. Superficially she was undeniably Leith. (Certainly more than her mother's Cyr side of the family tree, which had always seemed, by-and-large, secondary – a portrait of far fewer shades painted with far fewer broad and hasty strokes.) Erin had her father's eyes. She had his sister's (her Aunt Shannon's) smile, though not her laugh. And as for her height? Well, rather than ever deigning to consider whatever lanky frames may have been lurking around the Cyr ancestry, Leith wisdom – with which her mother was enthusiastically complicit – actually posited a second cousin once removed as the source for her turning out '*a bit uncharacteristically tall*'. Often it seemed like these assigned attributes were the extent of her contribution to her father's lineage. That she was no more than a set of comparatives to the relatives who had come before her, with nothing of her own making a contribution or addition.

Erin's brother Nate, on the other hand, had never felt this way. Never felt it, never considered it, never entertained the need to explore his sister's take on it. Because Nate Leith found life painlessly easy, steering a path that offered next to nothing in the way of resistance. At university he had earned well the crown of his year's most notorious carouser, anecdotally infamous for his every-weekend alcohol-induced candour and his lack of correctness, be it political or social. All of this was forgiven because of her brother's sheer and effortless brilliance when it came to academics. He made the Dean's list every year. Graduated his commerce degree in the top percentile – a semester early no less. Then it was a Masters abroad (Auckland no less), followed by a fellowship at Cornell, which was all that Erin's parents, aunts, uncles and grandparents seemed to care to know. Any whispers or concerns about self-destructive behaviour or damage to others around him was easily mitigated, if not outright dismissed. (Sadly, the *others* in question were, inevitably, a succession of wide-eyed co-eds who had suffered from the misguided notion that her brother's Straight A smile had been flashed exclusively for them.) The trail of heartbreak had actually started back in high school, but slithered to its full length in the dorm rooms and floor parties of every residence on campus, giving rise to delighted high-fives from the rest of the soccer team. (Yes, the bugger also made varsity.)

Paradoxically however, this frat-boy lifestyle would not follow him into the working world. Upon finishing his fellowship, Nathan – no longer Nate – had spun an abrupt hundred-eighty degrees into a dedicated and ambitious business professional. Within a decade he was fast-tracked to management, and then partner and CEO of a London, Ontario investment firm. Nothing but suits, payrolls, chamber of commerce meetings for him. Most attributed the transformation to Kelsey Ronson, his first-ever exclusive girlfriend-turned-wife. Trevor, of course, had claimed otherwise. Claimed he had always seen it coming. This despite the fact he and his cousin were in no way close. Nate and Trevor had long since ceased seeing the point of one another. (A corporate investor and a used-record store owner – Gordon Downie himself couldn't have lyric-written the two of them into sitting down for a pint.)

"It's not her, Cuz. Honestly, it's just a life-station thing," he had declared over coffee one day. "And that fucking unquenchable competitive streak of his."

"Okay, genius, show your work."

"Simple. Nate ... sorry, Nathan ... is doing exactly what he has always done. He's doing what he believes is expected of him. But his jam is to make sure it's done to the bloody hilt. The *nth* degree ... beyond everybody else around him. So it may be all double-Windsor knots and briefcases, but it's really still the same old conquest shit he did back in his dorm party days."

It had been an intriguing opinion – mostly because it dovetailed with her own take on this stranger that happened to be her brother. The truth was, when it came to Nate, she had always been at odds, without even trying – she with her lacklustre BA in English followed by an uninspired trip to teachers' college, he with all his upwardly mobile goals all lined up and knocked down like a row of dominoes. It had long seemed so pointless to hold up her life in comparison against his. A fool's errand. Nevertheless, it was a rabbit hole she had often found herself falling into, usually during either the dreaded anticipation or numbing aftermath of some Leith family function. Unavoidably, it would always leave her feeling as if she were tethered to a post from which the pendulum of all her brother's achievements swung, and there she was – strapped to his life, clutching at air as he sped by, this way and that.

Thank God for Trev. He was and had always been the one extended family member whose kinship transcended the obligatory. When all the aunts and uncles and their other offspring had faded to once-a-year visits void of any meaningful association beyond the shared surname, Trevor had remained a constant. Like a sweater she never outgrew no matter how much life changed. Certainly he was the only candidate – amongst friends or family – she could ever imagine confessing her beach escapades to, and imagine the typically irreverent response ... the ensuing banter.

"So you're checking out women on the beach. Well that's pretty hot!"

"Really, Trev? That's all you've got?"

"Hey you know what? I say don't sweat it. I mean, sometimes you don't get to decide stuff like this. Sometimes stuff like this finds you."

Growing up the two had actually spent many a summer day at the beach themselves during those annual Leith family beach vacations. Indeed a great portion of her memories of those times featured Trevor and herself playing together ... stuffed into water wings, and floaties, paddling about on styrofoam boards, rounds of mini-golf, stops at the Dairy Queen. They had built sandcastles, kicked over sandcastles, body-surfed the waves from sandbar to sandbar, all under the nervous gaze of their mothers, who had instilled the love and fear of Lake Huron into their lexicon, with sobering warnings of undertows and stomach cramps.

Only once in their young lives had awkwardness intervened. When she was twelve, possibly thirteen. It was the first summer Nate was noticeably absent from their midst – busy as he was with the neighbouring cottage's kids. (The ones with the inboard motor boat, and the water-skis.) It had happened one afternoon towards the end of the holiday. Trevor's fruitless attempts to light and smoke one of his father's menthols had given way to teasing on her part, then a tugging match over the book of matches, so sure was Erin that she could do better. What followed was some sand-throwing in one another's general direction, *noogies* across the top of a headlock, and an attempted over-the-hip one-leg takedown with requisite wrestling commentary. But as they fell in a heap of mangled arms and legs, a hand had landed curiously on a recently formed breast where, to her mind, it had remained for too many seconds to plead a case of plausible deniability. She slapped at the side of his face and pushed him off. Then there was a moment of simply staring at one another expressionless – he with his knees drawn up, rocking slightly, she with arms crossed tightly across her chest, thumbs pinned in her armpits. For a moment he looked defiant, like he was going to challenge her to prove something different had just occurred. Something *on purpose.* But before that could happen, much to her own surprise, let alone her cousin's, she went on the offensive, crying out "oh yeah?" and grabbing at the front tie of his swim shorts. He spun away and jumped to his feet, leaving her in a heap on the sand, as he stood staring at his feet, droop-shouldered, arms straight at his sides, squeezing and un-squeezing his fists. After several more awkwardly silent seconds in this pose, he mumbled something that vaguely sounded like the word *sorry*, then sprinted off down the beach faster than she had ever remembered seeing him run.

~5~

With her sandals already off and in hand, she all but tiptoed across the cement out toward the rocks, very much wanting to call out a greeting, but reticent to do so. Erin had never profited from first impressions. She knew that. Whereas many cannot stand the sight of themselves photographed, and others recoil at the sound of their recorded speaking voice, she could not help being bothered at the thought of how she was generally perceived by others. Could often only cringe when she considered herself from their perspective. And it wasn't just one pervasive idiosyncrasy. It was from the way she walked into a staff meeting, a restaurant, a shop – so stiff in her efforts to appear anything but – to the way she fidgeted when she was nervous, her eyes incapable of relaxing as they darted around the room. It was the way she so often spoke too quickly, and rattled on in far more detail than a recipient's interest warranted. Erin had every reason to assume these deficiencies had been on display in full force on her last visit to the beach, and she had no doubt they were lining up to put in an appearance when she spotted the same lanky woman standing chest-deep out in the water just off the furthest boulder. She was facing the horizon, hands on hips, head tilted quizzically, as if straining in the haze of the afternoon to determine where the water ended and sky began. Erin was suddenly aware of her pulse racing ever so slightly and, to her surprise, a shiver – despite the heavy weight of the midday sun. *The good news is, the longer you just stand here, the longer it is before something embarrassing happens,* one of the voices pointed out.

She took a moment to scan the opposite direction, noting a half-dozen teenagers sprawled on the edge of the beach, all lying at haphazard angles in the sand, phones out, sunglasses on, so comfortable in their own skin. Her inner voice continued its charge, arguing that if body confidence in public was actually the reason for her hesitancy, surely she could have just stayed home, slipped into her newly purchased, higher-cut two-piece and read a book in the privacy of her own backyard. She could have scratched her literacy itch and achieved that overall tan-goal all at the same time – two birds, one stone. She shivered again, colder this time, but held her ground, reaching out with her toes to kick at the lapping waves and watch the droplets splash into the sunlight. Because all rationalizations aside, one thing had made itself clear. Whatever she was feeling ... whatever she was now trying to live, or re-live or catch up to, the water was honestly proving to be an integral component. The sensation of cutting through the surface, slick as an arrow. And yes, maybe being out in public amidst this display of bodies, many more lithe and fit than she had or would ever feel – maybe that was part of the deal. Maybe as much a part as the smooth contour of her rock under her legs, and the glorious touch of the light summer breeze that tempered the sun toasting her forehead and shoulders. Strangely there was a relief in realizing this ... a silencing of the voices inside, at least for the moment. It was a sense of permission to carry on and it arrived in the form of yet another shiver. The good kind this time.

She unfolded her towel, anchoring three of the corners with her sandals and a paperback, then stretched out on her rock, looking out between her freshly painted toes to see the woman now wading back towards her. The woman waved. Erin responded with a smile, and called out a hello.

"So nice," the woman said, climbing up on her rock, and reached for a tank top, which she used to pat her shoulders dry before edging herself back to lean against another rock and let the sun finish the job.

"I'm Erin."

The woman dropped her sunglasses from her hairline and

smiled back. "I like your suit," she said.

"Thanks. Yours too. Great colour on you."

The woman drew up her knees and rubbed her hands down her shins. "I think I'm happy with it," she replied with a grin. "Now that I survived the wax job. I'm such a baby." She nodded toward the paperback. "What are we reading?"

Erin picked up the book with her free hand, for some reason flipping it to consider the back cover. "I don't know. I grabbed it from the library last week. Some sort of magic-realism I think, but I actually haven't really got into it yet. Are you a reader?"

The woman opened her mouth to reply, but held it there wordless until a grin crossed her face. She grabbed her sunglasses from her nose and bounced over to sit next to Erin.

"I have an idea," she said.

"Okay?"

"No, hear me out. We're at that point in the conversation where I ask you where you're from. Whether you're from here in town, or vacationing. And you ask me what I do for a living, and so on and so forth ... right?"

"I guess–"

"So ... speaking of books," she reached for Erin's paperback and fanned through the pages. " I read one a while back where a guy is training a group of people, I think at a counselling centre – maybe. Anyway, he makes them all introduce themselves without making any reference to careers or jobs or college or family history."

"Interesting, I guess."

The woman shrugged, dropping the book back down beside Erin's towel, losing her place in the process. "It was just this little tangential part of the plot, but I kind of liked the idea, you know? It takes away the need to brag or oversell ... nobody lording anything over anyone else. You don't have to worry about coming across too successful, or not successful enough ... too rich, too poor. Too this, too that."

She hopped up onto her knees, and faced Erin. "Should we try it?"

Erin felt her shoulders shrug.

"Great," the woman said. Clapping her hands, and jumping to her feet, she grabbed Erin by the elbow and pulled her up as well. "But one more rule," she said, her eyes dancing back and forth between Erin's. "We do it out in the water."

"What?"

"Come on ... swim with me," she called back as she dove off the boulder, resurfacing with a flip to her back, her gaze skyward, her arms back over her head as she windmilled away from the shore.

~

"You mean you just go there all on your own?"

Erin nodded out the café window and cradled her tea, her feet folded up under her, knees pinned together. "Because if it were me, I'd just bake like a ham. I mean, that's why I moved the flowerbeds to the shady side of the house. Trust me, it wasn't for the marigolds' sake."

"The water cools you off," Erin explained, suddenly wishing she hadn't given in to the need to call someone and share. But given the subsequent events of her afternoon, the urge had simply been too strong not to tell someone – anyone – at least a measured portion of how she had been spending her time lately. And since Trevor had not found it in his heart to reply to any of her emails, or to answer her three text messages, against Erin's better judgement a spur-of-the-moment consolation candidate was called in.

Erin had known Audrey Capito since tenth grade. Always a

willing conversationalist, and ever eager to get things off *your* chest, Audrey lived to be the one who delved deeper than all others, understood your trials just a degree or two more than anyone else. The proud ear of many, she always had an arsenal of confidences – with veiled references to each and every one of them always at the ready.

"Well, it is good exercise I suppose?" she said absently as she leaned over their table, one hand glued to the mug she had yet to sip from, the other slowly leafing through a home decorating magazine she had grabbed from the counter. "I mean, you've always liked to stay healthy, haven't you?" she added, as she tapped her finger on one of a succession of photos of bedroom renovations. "I mean, as long as it's nothing completely compulsive. Like my neighbour Camille a few years back, remember? When she got into her problems with the casino. The stories I could tell there ..."

The stories she could tell. Audrey had hinted at so many anecdotes with this phrase, that over the years Erin had learned to accept it for the benign claim it was – a close second as a go-to phrase to the even more frequent *I don't mean to pry*, which was always, inevitably, followed by a very intentional act of prying. (And should any of her lengthy narratives include one of her iconic *I was speechless* tags ... well, best settle in.) *The stories she could tell.* Well, tell some already! How many times had Erin wanted to lob that back across the table? Or, in theory at least. In truth the impulse usually only occurred after the fact. Because despite the shortcomings of Audrey's counsel, Erin could still always count on the utility of their get-togethers. For years it had been every Sunday afternoon. But once her son Terrell finally made the rep hockey team, with weekends tied up on road trips, practices and fundraisers and off-season fitness sessions, their ritual had regressed to something much more intermittent.

"The stories I could tell," Erin mimicked as she pulled out of the coffee shop parking lot, the bulk of her planned disclosure left unspoken, trumped in the introductory stages by a rant about the overwhelming numbers of vacationers on the beaches this summer, with their big cumbersome tents and their barbecues, and all that litter. "Whole extended families too," (which apparently was a negative). "Who wants to sit out there with all that?"

"Maybe I do, Audrey," she had snapped back unexpectedly, grabbing her belongings and heading for the door. "Maybe I like a good crowded, littered beach."

Well, what were you thinking anyway? Audrey? With this bit of news? Really? The questions were valid ones. Even accepting for the moment her fleeting desire to – what? ... confess? ... explain herself? Legitimize her actions? Why her? Why a woman who, but for two years away getting a business diploma at the nearest possible college, still lived in the same town where she was born and raised? *Maybe because you live all of one town over from where you were born and raised?* At least the voice had calmed down a bit and raised the point more gently ... even phrased it in the form of a question ... like a friend, almost.

It wasn't often the case.

~

The breeze died to barely a whisper, the lake's surface pulled smooth as a top-sheet. They had been in the lake for a better part of an hour, drifting on their backs letting whatever hint of invisible current rotate them in slow indiscriminate circles as they shared stories and water alike.

First had been favourite foods. The woman confessed she had a sweet tooth. Anything chocolate, milk or dark, though lately, she said, it was a craving that came and went more sporadically. Erin was all about red meat and potatoes, but did acknowledged her culinary tastes had been slow to diversify from the protein-starch-vegetable regimen of her childhood.

"No tofu adventures for you then?"

"Well once I got away to school–"

"Um, remember the rules–"

"Nope. Not saying where. Not saying for what–"

"Atta girl."

"But I was really, really into curries for a while ... and Mexican ... and God, if I had just known about cilantro back then–"

"I was a fat kid," the woman blurted out, and Erin shot a dubious glance. "No, really, I was. Trust me, I'm not one for fake self-deprecation. There, that's another bit about me. I can't stand false modesty. All through high school, I sat behind this girl – Susan Walker. Brightest one in the school. Or at least the most motivated. Or the one who needed the most affirmation? I don't know, maybe that's a bit too bitchy. Anyway, she always had the top mark on every assignment in every class ... every year. And still it didn't matter. Because there'd she'd be, walking out of an exam, absolutely sure she had failed ... *just sure of it.* I hated that shit. Still do. Just, own who you are, right? I mean look at us. We're out here proud enough, aren't we? Rocking the two-piece? What are you, five-seven?"

"Closer to eight actually."

"Me too. And I mean, we look good, right? Not model photo-shoot material, I know. Trust me, I'm not deluded. Christ, I passed a woman sun-tanning back near the parking lot. Two kids beside her playing in the sand, and she's rocking a thong. Mind you, if I had her glutes I just might be doing the same. There, that's one more bit. I'm gonna try a thong one day. Just once." She stood up in the water and peered over her shoulder down her back, playing and pulling up on the band of her suit until she noticed Erin had looked away.

"TMI?"

In truth, Erin's momentary silence owed more to the shock of hearing herself included in such a favourable description. Nevertheless she did find herself steering the conversation away from anatomical matters, focusing instead on artistic sensibilities. She confessed a love for bright bold decorative colours, and described for the woman how she had recently redone her living room in a rich aquamarine that made the white trim around doors and window frames pop really effectively. Similarly the deep green in her hallway the previous spring, and golden yellow for the kitchen the year before. She shared her fear that she would one day tire of these stronger hues. That she would succumb to some toned-down life stage that coerced her toward muted and subdued walls and trim – that endless shuffle through a sea of swatches of forty or fifty different shades and names for off-white ... eggshell, mist, spring snow, winter's eve, parsnip ...

"I get bold," the woman replied as she pulled her feet under her to stand a moment, her hand reaching out to find Erin's forearm for balance. "I have to listen to my music with the sound up full. I mean, the parts a band want quiet, they'll record quiet right? But when a tune is rocking full bore, I need it to wash right over me, you know?" A couple of fingers lingered for a second, absently tapping a rhythm out on Erin's wrist. "Sorry," she said, catching sight of Erin's glance. Immediately she pushed off the lake bed, propelling herself away with a couple of solid backstrokes. Erin followed along behind.

They would stay in the water a while longer, sometimes floating side by side ... touching down again from time to time to stand and skim their hands across the surface. At different points, both took a turn gliding back close enough to shore to climb around some of the partly submerged rocks just off the water's edge, and to glance about at the comings and goings of other would-be swimmers and beach hikers – a silently agreed-upon break in their entertainment. An intermission of sorts.

Eventually Erin started in on her love of books, explaining how so much of her literary preferences involved tales of ordinary lives in extraordinary situations. The everyday mixed with the exotic, she explained. She firmly believed that good CanLit was at its best when spiced and flavoured with hyphenated settings and characters. Afro-Canadian, French-Canadian, Sino-Canadian, Indi-Canadian ... stories that took everyday characters she could see in herself and flung them through space and time on some adventure in the world at large. That's why she loved Ondaatje, she said. Who else could get the exotic deserts of Egypt and the town of Brighton, Ontario into the same narrative so seamlessly? Then she testified about her own on-again, off-again relationship with the process of creative writing.

"I'm even trying a writing class at my town library ... sorry, does that count as reference to schooling?"

"I'll allow it," the woman replied floating up face to face, her grin a mere fraction above the surface of the water.

"I haven't quite got comfortable with it yet, though. Almost everybody there is older ... retired folk working on some family memoir or church history. Funny thing is, there was a time when I would have found that stuff interesting. But now it just makes my chest feel heavy."

The woman studied Erin's expression, noting how her gaze had suddenly gone distant. "There's nobody at all your age?" she asked after a moment's pause.

"Well, one or two maybe ... and one much younger too. But with them it seems even more ... I don't know ... claustrophobic? Like they're trapped in the same poetry of self-discovery week after week. Like they're writing in quicksand."

The woman stood once more, this time reaching out her hands

to invite Erin to do the same. "And what about you?" she said, wiggling her fingers, then pulling Erin up in front of her, her chestnut eyes dancing back and forth. "What do you like to write about?"

Erin shrugged. "I think I just want to lose myself."

"... in a good book."

"... of my own design, yeah."

"You want to be someone else?"

Another shrug.

"Someone other than my new swimming friend?" She felt the blood flood into her cheeks, shrugged her shoulders a third time and averted her eyes. "Okay then ... other than the woman with the bold house colours?"

"The bold colours probably *are* me trying to be someone different. Maybe swimming here too ... if that makes any sense."

The woman found Erin's hands and cradled them, palms resting on top of her own. And then she kissed her, her mouth barely parted, gently and faintly hugging the tip of Erin's upper lip. It lasted about four seconds, after which the woman immediately swam back to shore and climbed up over the rocks, grabbing her shirt and shoes as she went.

Only after she was gone could Erin – still waist-deep in the lake – take in any other sounds around her. The hovering gulls squawking high overhead, the distant drones of outboard engines, a Jet Ski, a bike chain changing gears up on the pathway ... the squeals of children playing at the water's edge. And only then did she think to look about to see who, if anyone, had been watching them. Not that she really needed to be concerned. The height of the breakwater had effectively blocked the sight lines of any potential spectators. Like the quartet of teenage boys on the leeward side of the dock hand-paddling air mattresses in a race, or the three volleyball games in full swing on the sand well beyond them ... the pair of vacationers neck-deep in water locked in their own embrace ... and out beyond them all, standing at the edge of the breakwater in a crisp, bright pant suit, an elderly woman with her hair done just so, clutching another balloon in her fist.

~

Just as she nears the lamppost at the end of the seawall, a double wave will interrupt the rhythm of her stride and send her reeling. In desperation she will lunge for the stanchion, but the force will flip her feet from beneath her and she will be awash, frantically scrambling and scratching, first for the base of the light, next a docking ring, before finally finding purchase, clinging onto a mooring post.

Only then will she hear voices that are not her own, coming from the shoreline behind her, calling for her to hang on – that help is on its way. Somewhere back beyond the panic, in the recesses of her mind, she will understand this. And yet, once the voices arrive she will refuse to let go. She will beg them to leave her be – even though one of the voices is calling her by name, chastising her for venturing out on the dock and risking her life in the first place. She will try to drown out this voice in particular with her own screams. Then she will break down in tears, pounding on the chest of a man who has grabbed her by the shoulders to drag her back to safety.

~6~

Erin drove straight home from the coffee shop, pausing in the driveway to cherish a couple of more precious seconds of the indefinite. Wasn't that how this had started, after all? The long way around to the grocery store, the pharmacy, a fabricated errand here, something needing picking up there. That was what had segued into the longer aimless car rides – windows down, radio up. The solace of being nowhere in particular ... no *one* in particular.

She cast her eyes towards her house, peering up to the second floor window where her sleep was now so routinely interrupted – the voices relentless in reminding her night after night how unsettled her life was. For so long she had managed to keep those voices – that restlessness – at bay. So life could keep churning away.

She yanked the keys from the ignition. Paused once more and let out a full sigh, emptying her lungs completely before drawing in a brand new breath. Then grabbed the grocery bag from the back seat. Not a full shop, just a few cold cuts and some bread and cheese. And coffee. His text had said they were out of coffee.

Chapter Two

~

What are the things that weigh her down? The things that when absent put movement back into her days, a joy and lightness to the motion of her stepping across the sand, splashing through the leading edge of a washing wave. Because it's clear that for these visits to be freeing and deliberate and languid and all the things they joyously are ... much of her simply cannot make the trip. Is it a ring... or a wallet? Identification? A surname even?

Can she remember the first time she stripped them all away? Was it was a sudden epiphany, or completely by chance? Was it the surf's first dance across her toes that caused her head to pop up from a litany of texts and posts? The sight of endless jewelled wavelets playing with the sunlight, silencing all that preoccupied her thoughts? Did she race back to her car to jettison her phone right then and there ... likewise a handbag, and the shoes she had been carrying, before making her way back to the shore? Her footsteps now lighter and eager – like those of someone anxious to get somewhere? Or perhaps someone anxious to flee from where they have been?

~

~1~

Erin Leith has been married to Ross Morton for twenty-three years. They were wed on a bright and sunny afternoon in May when they were both just 21 years old – the current age of their only child, a daughter named Avery.

Ross was the older of two sons born to Willard and Leyla Morton. Willard had moved his family north from Kitchener when he secured work in the maintenance department at the Nuclear Power Plant in the fall of 1976. Ever the pragmatist, (something which he proudly attributed to a Scottish heritage), he searched nearby towns for the most affordable family home, willing to sacrifice proximity to the plant for a reduced price. He settled on a bungalow in the town of Wiarton, one hour to the north, with a beautiful view of the Niagara Escarpment and Colpoy's Bay out the kitchen window. His wife appreciated this, because ever since she was a child she had carried a strong compulsion to keep an eye on the water.

She was born Leyla Posner, first-generation Polish-Canadian. Her mother and father, along with two of her uncles, left Gdansk in 1945, during the relentless transition of their homeland from Nazi rule to the height of Soviet suppression. They had paid for passage in the hold of a freighter bound first for the UK, then spent four years in Lincolnshire before making the voyage to Ontario. All of the Posner men found work on lake freighters sailing out of Midland and Owen Sound. But whereas her uncles lasted only one season before turning their sights to inland jobs at an auto parts factory in Windsor, Leyla's father found his calling out on the water.

He would spend the rest of his working life on the boats, away from his wife and daughter nine months of the year. To her credit, Leyla's mother managed through most of that time span stoically – all alone in a small town of a country not of her birth, nor her mother tongue. Every year, however, her patience and nerves would wear threadbare by the time October and November rolled around. When the Great Lakes were still warm enough from a spent summer to mix with the cold fronts from the northwest and churn up the fiercest of weather. Leyla's 'forever' childhood image was of her mother glued to the chair that sat just below the wall-mounted telephone in the front hall, her head buried in her hands. It was a chair reserved for phone conversations – but, all too often during those later autumn months, reserved more for the long apprehensive waits between those phone conversations – ship to shore – when The Lakes were stirred up so. It was a strategic location in other respects too, close enough to the door to answer any potential news being delivered in person, but also within earshot of the radio and its hourly weather reports, always rattled off quicker and with less sensitivity than should have been required – or at least that was Leyla's recollection.

No, autumns were not kind for mother and daughter. The joys that the season provided for the rest of the town were lost on their household. Supposedly vibrant fall colours were merely a promise of deteriorating weather to come – nothing more than a reminder that the foliage in question would soon dull to a lifeless brown, and be ripped unceremoniously from branch and limb to scatter across their lawn or wedge mulch-like under their front stoop, and within lattice beneath the side verandah. Raked, piled and neatly disposed on every other lawn and driveway on their street, on their property it would remain in cluttered chaos because Mr. Posner was not home ... and he would not be home until a week before Christmas at best. More than likely not before at least one decent blow of snow had riled Superior and Michigan and Huron.

And as it turned out, it was, in fact, a day in early December when the news that they had for years so dreaded, finally arrived.

Leyla would actually strike the specific date from her memory, unable to pin it down more precisely than 'somewhere between the third and the sixth'. This would always puzzle her, given how she would forever retain so many other details with such vivid precision. The bluish ink of the late afternoon sky as she had trotted up the walk from school. The piercing wail as she had opened the front door to find her mother spread across the floor, the telephone receiver dangling down the wall. And then the particulars of the ship's demise. Her father's boat had been caught up on a shoal in northern Lake Michigan. Stranded by weather and hobbled by engine failure, they were told, he had been tasked with helping keep the boiler running until the storm broke and help might reach them – help that would not arrive in time. From that day onward Leyla Posner would always have a complicated relationship with the Lakes. Infatuation on one hand, for her father had truly loved the open water, and she in turn had truly loved her father. But also anger. And resentment as well. It was after all, this first love of her father's that had ripped him away from her and her mother. Left them to pine for him alone in death, much as they had while he was alive.

So one would be forgiven for assuming Leyla Morton, nee Posner, would grow up wanting no part of living and raising her son in a waterside town overlooking Georgian Bay. However, Leyla Morton was not one to shy from her fears, and, over time, worked to make her peace with the lakes. To keep a careful watch on their currents and power. Even to develop – albeit years later – a certain respect for the windblown bay that bounded her home town. So much so that, many more years later, it would be Leyla Morton who would properly teach her daughter-in-law, Erin Leith, how to swim.

~

"Hey, Rinn, check this out," he called from the spare-bedroom-cum-recording-studio, pointing to the left screen of his double-monitor set-up, and tracing his hand across the graphic depicting yet another guitar track for his latest song. "That bugger there was fifteen takes in the making," he declared, sliding the cursor over the jagged edges of the music's visual rendering. With a click of his mouse, the image expanded out like an accordion, transformed from spiked blotches of pixels into a single line of rounded crests and troughs. Then with another click, the part folded up once more.

"It looks like trees reflected on a lake," she said, knowing it was a comment she had made many times before.

"Yes, I know. Or a fish."

She heard the annoyance in his tone, the result of him inferring disinterest on her part. And he was not mistaken. She would not even contest the point if he actually ever called her on it. But until then ... well, the bloody thing actually *did* look like a fish. Whether he acknowledged it or not, the fruits of his pained labours to add an extra guitar line to a song he had been working on for the past four months ... a song he had penned, sung, strummed, drummed to, harmonized on, finished recording, listened to, deleted, started over again ... to her eye that guitar part, no matter how enriching a contribution it might be, would still, like those that had gone before, resemble the elongated skeletal system of a northern pike.

Once upon a time, the object of his dedication had been her. Briefly. Before the delineations and domestic patterns of work and raising a daughter set in. When his job managing the arena was still new and a little bit daunting. The ice-making procedures, Zamboni maintenance, the scheduling of competing constituents ... hockey moms, figure-skater moms, public skaters, old-timer leagues. But after a few years, once these skills had been mastered and repeated ... well, routine had never been his friend. So he answered his first call to *upgrade* – as he had put it. Headed back to school for a teaching degree. He thought biology was his ticket initially, until it was, in turn, trumped by a sudden obsession with meteorology, brought about after studying a couple of units on the subject in a course on climate change. That, of course, brought about his storm-chasing phase, complete with all the electronic scanners and radios for the second car that their paycheques could not really afford.

Such was the Ross Morton way. An enterprise worth doing needed an all-in, no-stones-unturned approach. It was something Erin had long acknowledged in her husband, originally with awe, then incredulity, then for the past few years, if she was honest ... with disdain. It wasn't the succession of pastimes themselves, as much as his constant need for her to match the enthusiasm for each and every new endeavour that arrived to preoccupy him – something she could no longer even feign to summon. Not when she knew in her heart that another one-eighty turn, and another obsession, lay just around the corner. It was a pattern that, for Erin, carried a cumulative effect. Like a series of floats and marching bands crashing into one another in a parade already far too congested for her ever to get a chance at being co-marshal, the route simply too narrow for any of her passions to leave the curb. So she was simply left to be party to her husband's predictable and constant childlike exuberance marching this way and that – witness to his seemingly heartfelt belief that each new interest was actually ... finally ... *the one* endeavour he had been waiting for. That thing that had just been waiting to make him tick.

Lately Erin had begun wondering how much sooner her apathy towards Ross would have arrived, had it not been for Avery. Because for a good decade or more, her daughter had been the saving grace – the buffer that had spared her from being the lightning rod for her husband's bolts of inspiration. They had always been very close, Ross and Avery, sharing a certain playful deductive intelligence, with endless afternoons spent huddled over cribbage pegs, chessboards, and a procession of other games requiring a good degree of strategic and tactical thinking. It had started early in their daughter's life, when bed time tuck-ins had eschewed story books in favour of word games and brain-teasers.

"*One more, Dad, please?*"

"*Just one ... then lights out.*"

"*YES!*"

"*Okay ... a boy breaks his arm playing soccer and his father rushes him to the nearest hospital. X-rays show that the boy will need an operation to set the bone–*"

"*Gross!*"

"*Ah but ... there's a problem. The surgeon walks into the operating room, takes one look at the boy and says, 'I can't operate on this child ...he's my son.'*"

"*Too easy Dad ... the surgeon is the boy's mother.*"

"*That's my girl.*"

For years Avery was also the sponge for her father's interests, the catcher's mitt for his passions – whatever they might happen to be at the time. But unfortunately for Ross (and Erin) young daughters turn into teenagers – independent units often with far more mitigated levels of curiosity and zeal. And once Avery was out of the house, off on her own in university ... well, deep down in her heart Erin always knew she would never prove a viable alternative.

As near as she could pinpoint, her indifference had started in earnest with her husband's music-fetish, building like a crescendo – if indeed indifference could actually do such a thing – through all its varied iterations. It began when the Rotary Club started putting on concerts in the arena, exposing its manager to the world of show business. One of those shows was a completely acoustic set put on by none other than the front man of The Guess Who. Two guitar purchases and a year and a half of lessons later, Ross himself was signing up for open mics put on by the local folk music club.

Which led to signing up for the club's executive. Which led to more exposure to singer-songwriters. Garnet Rogers, Connie Kaldor, Valdy ... soon he was the club's treasurer. Soon he was offering to store the club's PA gear, and signing up for more night courses on concert sound, his detailed approach informing him about each and every slider, each and every input and output of the 16-channel soundboard, which under his tenure was soon upgraded to 24. Then digital. Ross sometimes booked himself as the opener on nights when the club entertained a touring act, and proudly framed and mounted pictures taken of him playing in support of *Blackie and the Rodeo Kings* at the club's twenty-year anniversary show ... another when he opened for *Mill Run.*

Erin rarely attended. She found the patrons too ... well, too *something.* It was a completely intangible kind of *something* that she knew she could never adequately describe, and was reasonably assured she shouldn't dare try. The closest she came was during one of her coffee-conversations with Audrey.

"The folk club's his toy, not mine," she had divulged, "And I know this is going to sound awful, but there are just way too many people there that are ... well, like Ross."

The look back from her friend had not been charitable so Erin left it at that, not bothering to clarify how she found the folk club to be full of annoyingly eager souls, unschooled in the finer social skills of personal space. And it's not like she hadn't tried to come to terms and accept these people as they were. Be the supportive wife. *('Welcome aboard, Erin ... we're a club with an active membership of a few dozen-odd people ... and I do mean odd.')* She even tried hauling Trevor along for the ride once, given his love of live music.

"Sorry, Cuz. The music's okay but, I mean, some of those people are just way too intense."

She understood. Too many people with too many unsolicited

opinions on too many subjects. Similarly, too many unsolicited personal histories delivered with an unfathomable assumed interest. Too many hour-by-hour accounts of vacations recited with courtroom accuracy. Had she thought it any use, Erin would have tried to explain to Audrey that the problem with the folk club was, despite its mandate to stage artistic expression, it was full of *folks* more interested in the *how* than the *what* of the music. More intent to discuss the make of the guitar a performer played, than the song that came out of it. More obsessed with the fact they had been to a certain town a singer had mentioned in a song, than the song itself. More focused on how the strumming pattern on a particular ballad was exactly the same as they had come up with themselves ... a song about Louis Riel's Rebellion they had been working on for four months. It was as if they only looked for themselves in what they took in. Affirmation posing as art. (Tools of the trade posing as a fish or a tree's reflection.)

"You started dinner?" she called from the downstairs bathroom.

"In a minute," he said to the screen. "Just want to ..."

She listened a moment to see if the response would finish, then reached behind to untie the strings of her swim top – pulling it out from under her shirt and tossing it in a nearby hamper. She grabbed a scrunchy from the vanity and headed for the kitchen, leaving *The Ballad of Louis Riel*, much like her husband's response, to trail away unheard.

~2~

Samantha Page

We're a family of four renting a cottage the second week of August. Looking for recommendations for good dining options. Will have a gluten-free eight-year-old, and a recently turned vegan teenager in tow. Wondering how limited our options will be.

Minah Govier

Frank's Grill on the beach has some gluten-free items. Not sure how big a selection but as long as your vegan teen loves fries, you shouldn't have a problem :)

Seth Shields

Try Livingstone's Marketside as you head into town. They'll have a bunch of gluten-free.

Samantha Page

Thanks for the tips. Fries probably not a go ... probably cooked in animal fat, I'm being told (with rolled eyes). Might have to stock up on the groceries ahead of time ... lol. She'll be fine, as long as the water's warm and she's got room to stretch out on the beach and ignore her parents ... lol

Erin clicked off her phone as her writing group came to order. They met in the town library, down a side hall from the front desk in what was advertised as a conference room. Erin had always found the description on the generous side, given how the space barely accommodated their seven strong around a modest rectangular oak table.

Doreen Lemke was passing out copies of a short story she had been working on. Standard procedure was to email any submissions to the group a few days in advance, so members would have a chance to go over them before the session. However, Doreen claimed inspiration had struck only the night before and she could not resist sharing the brand new piece. And as *de facto* facilitator of the group, if anyone could bend the rules a bit for creativity's sake, it was Doreen. "It just started coming in waves, once I got rid of the narrator's voice in the first person," she explained, as she dealt out her prose.

The next few minutes were spent in uncharacteristic silence as everyone perused the draft – a short fantasy segment entitled *Horse Play*. Taking place in a thoroughbred racing stable, its premise held that all the horses envied those among them who had finished in last place during any of the day's races, for they had the good fortune of heading straight back to the paddock to enjoy a manger full of oats, and a drinking trough of fresh clean water. The winners, on the other hand, were forced to stay behind to have unwanted blankets slung over their sweaty shoulders while giddy ladies in flowered hats surrounded them and photographers' camera flashes exploded in their eyes.

There were the standard commendations from the more supportive members of the group. The first was from a woman named Yvonne, who was always careful to lead any comments with something positive, and to phrase any criticisms in the form of a question. Next was a brief thumbs up and affirmation from Erin's favourite, a teenager named Natasha, who always sat at an angle in her chair with her knees drawn up under her chin. She usually wore black jeans and a white shirt – neutral tones that Erin thought made her shock of purple hair pop so beautifully across her forehead. Throughout each session, Natasha's pencil never stopped doodling, as she added to a collage of graffiti across the front of her journal. Erin loved to watch the random patterns emerging from under the young woman's hand, an appendage seemingly detached from the class itself ... free from the *work* of writing as it created away independently and naturally … all on its own.

The woman to the far side of Natasha followed in turn. She was an effusive and jovial soul, whose good nature suffered only from an acute sense of over-familiarity – her comments burdened by the assumption that everyone in the room moved in exactly the same social circles as she.

"Really nice job, Doreen," she said. "Of course Bob could help you with some of the horse details, having grown up with geldings on the farm."

Bob, who had come up frequently in the woman's comments before, was her husband – or so Erin assumed. Similarly, from the ensuing extraneousness, it sounded like someone named Ruth, who now lived at the farm, might be her husband's sister. And the twins whom she mentioned tangentially – they had finally found an apartment together next to the Dollarama, which was going to be tricky since only one of them was working full-time at the moment – were Ruth's daughters? Erin had never actually learned this woman's name – first or last. Lengthy details about her life, yes. Her quilt guild's retreat plans. The local Presbyterian church history she hoped to write one day, because both her and Bob's parents were married there. And that the stone used to build that church was quarried from the back of a farm that her great-grandfather had cleared ... but not her name.

Moderate commentary continued around the table like ripples retreating from a splash, until even the most polite of opinions had faded away. That was when Avril Lawrence dropped her pen and folded her hands. Avril rarely participated in the give-and-take of ideas amongst the group, preferring to wait for the opportunity to deliver unabated what she believed would certainly be the most definitive word on whatever the topic was at hand.

"I'm not sure in an anthropomorphic piece like this, that all the detail about harnesses and tack are a necessity. Surely the implied commentary on human competitiveness is what's at the core."

A man named Barry, one of only two males in the group, went a step further, stating he could not accept the *anthropomorphy* of the piece in and of itself. Erin did not bother trying to catch why. Over the course of a dozen or so weeks she had not seen Barry submit even one piece of his own for review. And while it was true the same could be said of Erin herself, she could at least be satisfied she didn't come across like a hyper-critical contrarian who took great pleasure in shooting down other people's shortcomings with a quiver of literary terms and phrases, all launched in annoyingly condescending tones.

"You should probably know that this is a group that often likes to talk *about* writing far more than actually practising the craft itself," Doreen had whispered candidly at the conclusion of Erin's very first session. Erin liked Doreen. A retired librarian from the city, she was the antithesis of Barry. Effective and temperate in her remarks. The right mix of encouragement and advice. "Anything close to showing us, Erin?" she would ask quietly after each meeting, then follow it up immediately with a, "No pressure though ... whenever you're ready." Without Doreen Erin doubted she would have continued with the group. Doubted the group would survive at all. Doreen was the glue – without question.

Erin glanced at her phone for the time. 1:45. *I know what you're thinking,* the voice in her head interrupted. *You're thinking if Barry would shut the fuck up, you could still get out to the lake for an hour or so.*

~3~

The woman stood, chest-deep in the water in between the two biking man-boys, her arms outstretched, her palms brushing the surface back and forth gently, as she had done with Erin the day before. She was listening to something Todd's well-built friend was saying, nodding and throwing her head back in laughter.

Erin was unsure what to do – whether to call out and interrupt the conversation, or wait for the woman to glance her way. She decided she would go for a swim by herself. Just a quick out-and-back, then, since it was already fairly late in the day, head for home. She pulled off her cover-up – a bold (for her) pink cotton tank borrowed from her daughter's dresser – kicked off her sandals and slid quietly into the waves. But right away her breathing was off. And her swimming stroke was tight. After a mere thirty metres or so, she turned back for shore, diving under to dolphin-kick her way back as far as she could in one long breath, stretching her lungs to their limits before finally emerging up through the glassy underside for a gasp of air.

"Are you ignoring me?" The woman stood with her hands on hips, and a playful smile across her face that faded as soon as she realized Erin wasn't reciprocating. "Hey, you okay?" she asked, reaching out a hand. Erin dropped her eyes down towards the water and mumbled that she was fine.

"Look, if it's about yesterday, I'm really sorry. Afterwards I got thinking, what the hell was I doing? I have no reason to assume you'd be into me ... maybe you're completely straight ... hell, maybe you're married. I mean, I didn't remember seeing–" She lifted up Erin's limp left hand, gestured toward the ring finger, with an apologetic look of disgust. "Shit ... I've completely screwed this up. You were just being nice letting me come swim with you, and I took it too far–"

"No, it's not your–"

"And then I see you down here by yourself. Of course you would completely be avoiding me. I've completely freaked you out and I am so fucking sorry. I guess when I just saw you here a few times, and you were so unbelievably–" She slapped her free hand on the water searching for the best word, "...graceful..."

The woman planted her hands back on her hips, flexing her shoulders and looking away, as she braced herself to hear Erin confirm her take on the situation.

"You think I'm graceful?"

The woman nodded. "When you swim. Totally."

They stood face to face in the water, momentarily silent, letting the tension recede out into the lake, before the woman asked once more for reassurance that she hadn't completely ruined the previous afternoon with the kiss. Erin shook her head, and shrugged. She wanted to say more. Even opened her mouth in the fleeting hope she could command the moment and fully describe the joyful ambiguity their encounter had occasioned – access the would-be writer inside and find the words that could somehow articulate how profoundly beautiful, and scary, and intimate, and impossible it had all felt. But these were uncharted waters for Erin Leith. These were emotions that drifted between the waves of accessible vocabulary. And in their stead she could only offer the shrug, which was followed by a grin, slight at first ... before giving way to a giggle. "I don't know ... I don't know," she whispered back, her laughter continuing until tears began to pool in the corners of her eyes. Seeing them, the woman reached forward, gathering Erin into her arms.

"I'm Meg, by the way," she said.

~

Other times Erin strongly suspected that it was Ross's mum who actually held her marriage together. Certainly it was a more intimate relationship than she had ever cultivated with her own mother. True, there was less baggage. Leyla had no agenda. She kept no ledger of duties performed or social functions neglected. There was no adjudication of career or examination of life stations. Furthermore their visits were blessed with the missing ingredient that eluded all the extended Leith family functions – free will. And what a refreshing addition it was, when set against her own family's obligatory annual Christmas, Easter and Thanksgiving events.

Erin welcomed any excuse to meet with her mother-in-law, regularly volunteering to take her shopping or to an appointment with a doctor or a lawyer. It was because the scales of their conversation – whether that conversation was trickling or flowing, small talk or an exchange of ideas – were always so effortlessly balanced. Erin never once felt the need to dissect content after the fact, or measure her mother-in-law's words for possible subversive subtext. And even when the chatting faded, perhaps after a longer day of errands, the ensuing silence could feel equally as rewarding. Which had everything to do with the woman's disposition. Erin loved the way Leyla's eyes would scan the roadside, humming a contented tune in almost a whisper, periodically pointing out what caught her eye, without commentary. Just a raised finger and nod at a passing willow, or a songbird perched on a wire. She could find such satisfaction in the smallest things. The simplest of details. This had always been the woman's calming allure – the thing that made Erin thirst to know more about her. She loved to hear her take on the old family stories – especially those about Leyla's mother back in Poland. Always brief and specific anecdotes, they nevertheless implied a complete continuum of family history – individual snippets illuminated along one long rippled thread. They were tales her mother-in-law was only too happy to tell and retell before those snippets – in the absence of any other willing audience – inevitably lost their time in the light of day.

"My mother had it much harder." This was often her introductory disclaimer. Erin first recalled hearing it on an evening walk – an outing that would grow into a weekly ritual for the pair – strolling the neighbourhood together as their respective dogs trotted alongside, inadvertently braiding their leashes together with their haphazard routes from driveway to driveway, hydro pole to hydro pole ... scent to scent. It had been a March night, just after the clocks had been turned forward, very early on in her marriage. In Erin's memory, it had been a mild sunny day. She could recall the street and sidewalk were bare and dry of winter's residual slush, and could picture the decaying snowbanks that had receded enough to reveal the first glimpses of spring grass along the edge of the street curbs.

"My mother was married at seventeen, and one year later she was on a boat for a country she'd barely heard of. Couldn't speak a word of English."

"And I'm sorry, I should know this ... your mom's name before she got married?"

"Sosinski."

"Right. Ross has gone over this dozens of times, you'd think I could get it straight."

"Ah don't worry about that, dear. I'll get out some photos when we get back to the house. You'll stay for some tea, yes?"

That cup of tea also proved to be the first of many. With family albums full of faded images, and the frayed, yellowed pages of family diaries at the ready, Leyla would relay tales of her mother's childhood. How she was moved from farm to farm and hidden when Poland was occupied during the war. How Nazi soldiers had found her hiding under the floor-boards in a neighbour's stable – as she had been instructed to do whenever German officers were reported nearby. It had been a successful strategy for almost three years, until a fateful winter morning. Concealed overnight in freezing temperatures, she had assumed the coast was clear and scampered from the foundation to thaw in front of the wood stove. But one of the soldiers had doubled back. Apparently, upon reflection, he had calculated that the amount of food in the larder, and the number of plates left out on the kitchen table was suspicious, given the young farm couple's insistence they lived all alone ... and that their second bedroom was merely for the hired farm hands during harvest. The soldier had returned just in time to find young Ewa Sosinski being wrapped in blankets from head to toe in the fight against a creeping frostbite.

She was put on a train all alone with papers to hand to the conductor indicating where she was to be sent – her own personal postage stamp, Leyla called it. Then she was shipped west into Germany to work as a housemaid for the wife of a high-ranking officer in Breslau.

From then on, and for the duration of the war, her childhood was an endless and arduous routine, scrubbing floors that had no foot traffic, making beds in chambers that housed no guests, washing dishes taken from shelves that had fed no dinner parties. Her mistress nevertheless screamed at her daily, chastising the speed at which she scrubbed and mopped and dusted, berating her in more of the German language than the girl could ever hope to pick up, though she would glean eventually, from the long mumbling monologues that bridged the woman's bouts of vitriol, that those cold, scoured halls had once seen grander and kinder times. There had been three sons. That much Ewa had determined from family pictures in the upper hall. She suspected that all three had been swallowed up by Hitler's plans, judging from the three locked bedroom doors at the top of the main staircase, and from the way the woman ignored her husband – an officer in the Reich – when he dropped by every few weeks, never staying more than a night. From the way she never once uttered the Fuhrer's name ... and, of course, from her lifeless eyes whenever the monologues paused and she stared into space ...

Erin would always hold that first night of story-telling in her heart. She would remember how Leyla had stopped mid-plot – actually interrupted herself – to put a hand out to pat her daughter-in-law's forearm. "*This* is the important stuff, dear" she said. "Not what my mama's maiden name was. Anyway, this business with names ... a girl can get lost in all that sometimes."

~

For the next hour they carried on with the previous day's game, first standing chest-deep in the waves, absently scooping handfuls of lake. Then, at Meg's suggestion, they went for a walk, back past the breakwater, the marina and its parking lot, down to the long crowded sandy shoreline of the beach proper, strolling along in front of the surf, sometimes moving up to weave in and around the city of beach chairs and blankets and bodies

"So you really didn't know how to swim until you were an adult?"

Erin shrugged, kicking at the lapping wavelets snaking across her path.

"But you're so strong in the water."

"Well, we vacationed up at the beach when I was a kid and we were always splashing around, so it's not like I wasn't comfortable. But no, it wasn't until my mother-in-law got a hold of me. She'd pack a lunch and we'd go down to the shore on the Georgian Bay side. Find a picnic table. Before we ate, she'd strip down to her skivvies, as she called them, and just jump right in. She always said, 'Anyone living around the water has to learn a proper stroke.'"

"Sounds like my kind of woman."

"It's kind of like she knew ..."

"Knew what?"

"Knew me. Knew that at the heart of it all, I was this basket case that needed to ..."

She stopped to paw at the wet sand with a toenail, shook her head, chastising herself for assuming that this deep a dive was warranted. *Really, how much of your self-analysis does an acquaintance really want to hear?*

"Needed to what?" Meg urged, and, when a reply wasn't immediate, placed a hand on Erin's arm and peeked out from over her sunglasses. "Erin?"

"To breathe ... she always just lets me breathe," the school teacher said quickly. "I mean, quite literally that's what she was always on about. Getting me to submerge myself right up to my neck so the water was just below my bottom lip. Making me inhale and exhale really slowly until my breath was nice and relaxed. 'The air's just as good here as up on dry land,' she'd say. Then she'd get me floating ... after that, I was ready to tread water and swim down to the bottom. She was always on me to pull with my arms long and full."

The anecdote came to a halt there. Had Erin completed it, she would have shared the part of the story where she promised her mother-in-law she would, in due course, pass all of these same water skills onto her own daughter. But this part of the tale had caught in Erin's throat. So instead, she let her words trail away into the breeze, glancing up to find Meg's face still smiling in the sunlight. She opened her mouth to say something else. Change topics by way of voicing an observation. Though here too, she hesitated.

"What is it?"

"You used my name."

"What?"

"A second ago. You called me Erin."

Meg shrugged and started ahead down the beach once more. "I couldn't tell you when I learned to swim," she called back over her shoulder. "Just always could, for as long as I can remember."

Erin watched her go, and for a moment was once again lost in the shape of her, taking in the sleek precision of her posture, her squared shoulders standing, seemingly unconcerned and daunted by the world around her. It was a moment that should have stayed perfectly frozen in the warmth of the day for far longer, were it not for the careless words that escaped her lips mere seconds later. For in that brief flash of drinking her in, Erin's upbringing and privilege conspired against her. Without thinking she took in the rich hue of Meg's skin tone, and the jet strands of streamlined hair nestled beneath frosted tips, through the filter of someone *other* – someone apart from her own. And though the words came out without a grain of malice or judgement, once uttered they could not be made unsaid. Perhaps the moment had occurred – ironically – because Erin felt so relaxed around this woman. Perhaps the absence of her usual default towards inhibition had done her a disservice. "Was that on one of the local reserves?" she asked.

The reaction was instinctual and immediate, there and gone before Erin had even taken a stride to catch up. Just the slightest hint of tension in those magnificent shoulders, a slight folding forward for just a split second, followed by a catch in the rhythm of her breath – a microscopic sigh as her gaze fell to the lake's surface. Then it was over. Pasting her original smile back on her face, the woman reached back with both hands and grabbed Erin by the wrists.

"You know the best thing about walking on the beach?" she said, pulling the school teacher out into the waves. "We can totally just disappear in the water anytime we want."

Chapter Three

~

Megan wipes down the lunch counter vigorously. It's a menial task from which she takes disproportional pleasure. Seeing the coffee rings and food smudges disappear with just a few strenuous passes of her dishcloth offers an irresistibly tangible satisfaction. Mowing lawns holds a similar appeal, with the effect between before and after an immediate accomplishment right there to see, a purpose undeniably met and closed for debate. She often thinks she could have been quite happy as a groundskeeper, whiling away her income-generating hours trimming grasses to a pleasing conformity, content in the process of advancing the crisp, clear cut-line of a mower's swath. At a country club maybe, a golf course – provided she was spared from interaction with the clientele. This is where the attraction of the fantasy stalls, amid conjured images of bulging mid-sections, stomachs that her imagination paints in garishly patterned polo shirts stretched tightly above well-hiked powder-blue shorts and knee-high socks – her take on the out-and-about recreational attire of the retired and would-be retired, outdated and generalized though it is, she realizes. But then again, even if she were to update the fashion choices, the essence of her perception would remain ... middle-aged men, gathered to be intentionally amongst their own – their own hue, their own beliefs, their own opinions, their own *kind*. She imagines that for them it is a place where they feel free from the constraints of progress brought on first and foremost, they believe, by the encroachment of other hues and opinions and beliefs. She can hear them as they lament their government's out-of-control policies on immigration and social welfare ... right from the moment they waddle out from behind the trunks of their luxury sedans, lifting sets of sparkling, pristine graphite shafts onto motorized carts, that will chauffeur them out across her freshly cut fairways where, shot after shot, swing after swing, they will further lament the burden of insurance rates, the burden of their tax bracket, the burden of political correctness, of cancel culture, inclusive language and the never-satisfied demands for rights from the margins of society. And they will exercise their freedom by punctuating these lamentations with particular words and phrases that the *run-amok world* no longer allows them to utter elsewhere. They will revel in their freedom to use these words and phrases with impunity, as they refer to all things *other* – races and creeds, gender and orientations. Because at the end of the day, they will do as they please. As always used to be *their* right ... whenever two or more are gathered in these names ...

The journey from coffee stain to golf green is a swift one in Megan's mind, the distance from mug to grass clippings to retired insurance salesmen covered in a mere handful of daydreaming seconds. *Must be nice playing golf for a living,* she once heard her boss Frank teasing a young sales rep who was dropping off condiment samples before heading to a corporate event on the links. *You don't want to play golf with the people I have to play golf with* was the stone-faced reply as the man headed back out the door. Was that memory influencing this particular mind journey? No, she decides quickly. It was merely confirming the route.

She is distracted by her shirt collar. The black polo with the Frank's Grill logo on the breast pocket is deemed mandatory attire for all serving staff. (Neither she or any of the other servers ever use the pocket. Being new to the industry Frank had ordered the style with the assumption his waitresses would keep a pad and pen there. It's an unnecessary contingency. A waste of funds, if indeed it did actually incur any additional cost.) But whereas the pocket is simply a pointless detail, the collar – specifically where the tag was stitched at the back – is truly an irritant, rubbing at the back of her neck, just below her hairline, agitating the skin, usually right when she has two armloads of food.

In reality, it's a small inconvenience. Most of her work day is too busy for wardrobe issues (or daydreams). In the height of summer especially, the hours pass quickly with uninterrupted orders from the half-dozen tables she is charged to serve. Often she wishes she could linger at each table a little more. Not merely in the transactional hope of garnering larger tips, but out of a genuine interest in her customers, a curiosity gathered from the residue of overheard conversations. A glimpse into the lives that have found their way serendipitously to her own tiny corner of the universe.

Today it's a study in juxtaposed perspectives from the successive parties at her first table next to the window overlooking the water. The 12:30 sitting – not that Frank's Grill actually dallies in such formality – consists of a trio of backpackers with strong German accents, but impeccable English. They hover leisurely over a single order of fries and three herbal teas, chatting with Frank about their travels all across the country, west to east ... extolling the dramatic virtues of the Rocky Mountains and the vast skyline of the prairies. However, what they confess as most breathtaking and unequalled in their collective experience is the never-ending inland waters of the Great Lakes. "Nothing is like it where we come from," says one. His friend across the table agrees. "Because let us be honest. We have all seen mountains in pictures or actual life. Also with oceans. But to have all this water inside your country." The third diner, a slight woman with long dirty blonde braids picks up the thought, extrapolating on the culture that surrounds the Lakes, assigning a specific and discernible charm to the coastal villages they have visited. "Like this one," she says, gesturing out the window towards a few of Pyette

Beach's quainter craft stores. "And everywhere, the people are so friendly."

Megan thanks them for their kind words. In instances like these she feels an almost proprietary pride for her town. And yet it's the same town where, an hour before, her regular group of four had sat with their daily coffee, decrying the very same geography, rebuking the decision of the ministry of natural resources to cordon off a section of the beach for the propagation of *a few bloody bird nests*. From first sip to last drop they had bemoaned the situation, before settling up with Megan, whom, despite her name tag and despite her having worked there the better part of five years, they seem to know only as *darlin'*. *Have to hurry for a noon tee time*, one says – (no shit).

Moreover, Pyette Beach is also the same home that Bobbi, their eighteen-year-old dishwasher, can't wait to break free of. The very same small shops, the same homespun salutations up and down the streets and storefronts, the everybody-knows-everybody intimacy that the German tourists received like a hug, are like shackles around her feet, pulling taut every time she dreams of bolting for the city. Toronto or Vancouver maybe. The promise of being blissfully unknown. A blank canvas. Megan understands the impulse completely, though at her age it demands a more tempered response. She checks the clock. In half an hour she can unclip her unread name tag, hang her shirt by its scratchy collar from the hook in the staff washroom, change into her swimsuit and leave her shoes at the car. The rest of the day will be hers.

~

~|~

Ignatius Goyette

Our family is coming up from the city for a day-cation at your Beach. We are looking for information on by-law restrictions. Specifically barbecues. Allowed or not? Likewise for pitching a tent. Yes or no?

Hank Lum

Barbecues are a hard no. Same goes for full tents, although canopies with open sides are allowed.

Jordyn Fryer

For some reason

Hank Lum

Jordyn Fryer so we don't get campers filling up the beach trying to overnight for free.

Zack in the Six

More likely the local morality cops don't want any happy endings going on behind those thin little strips of canvas! :)

Ignatius Goyette

I can assure you, the tent would just be for my mother in case of rain or wind. She's eighty-four.

Zack in the Six

Chill, dude. Just a joke.

Erin didn't run into Meg the next day.

In truth she hadn't been certain of making the trip to the water herself. The morning had started out so overcast, with the distinct possibility of the humidity of the past week breaking. But by noon the clouds had parted and the sun returned.

A half-hour into her afternoon she decided to forgo her usual swimming rock and once again stroll the beach. She started out ambling a similar route to the one she and Meg had taken the day before, but soon found herself diverging from the shore up into the dry sand and back again, for no other reason than to take in the temperature change on the soles of her feet, alternating between the cool packed ground at water's edge to the pleasing give of an infinity of sun-baked grains closer to the dunes. In the process, she was continually swerving around a steady onslaught of children proudly caked in batches of mixed mud that had been joyously dug, mounded up and rolled in. She noted the endless shouts and waving gestures of mothers herding toddlers in waterlogged diapers, steering their giggles and slapping feet back into the shallows amidst the sapling legs of less dedicated fathers, rooted to the sand, drinks in hand, chatting to one another ... occasionally offering cursory shouts in support of their spouses' efforts.

She was suddenly aware of so many things she had forgotten from her own years as a new parent – chiefly the deliberation that had been required for navigating a family vacation. And yet she strained to recall if there had ever been a time when she was as fevered in her approach as the parents she now witnessed looming over their young. True, there had been their camping trip to the

Laurentians. And the holiday out west. Those had required a considerable degree of planning. But those memories all seemed so distant now. Almost foreign. Inaccessible. In fact, she could not help noticing that the family units she was now nipping in and around – these people *from away*, sharing *her* sand – were actually the antithesis of her own current motivation for coming to the beach. Hers, she told herself, was at its heart borne of a longing for freedom. It was a shedding of life's distractions so she could be present to feel all she wanted to feel. But all around her was quite the opposite. Around her was baggage. Around her was testament to the burden of micro-plotting for every contingency. Large umbrellas cumbersomely wrestled out to the shore to mitigate the afternoon's glorious rays, most likely transported in an oversized wagon outfitted with loungers, folding chairs and stools, stacked in and around inflatable toys of varying sizes and shapes. Options for sports. Frisbees and footballs, volleyballs and baseballs ... a bat and gloves. Not to mention the blankets and the towels, the coolers with drinks and snacks, the selection of magazines, an iPhone. She found it rather liberating, dodging this universe of belongings with only her sandals in one hand, her T-shirt in the other. She felt a little bit enlightened. Maybe a little bit superior ... being *of* the beach, not just *at* the beach. And so she strolled on light-footed, content to let every noise meld into a pleasant drone, to be rinsed percussively by the gentle constancy of the lapping shore, slight though the wavelets were that afternoon. Then, slowly but irresistibly, the smells of her surroundings took over. With her eyes fixed on no one in particular, her ears occupied with the lake's rhythms, she breathed in the musky aggregate of oils and lotions that had climbed from the multitude and onto the breeze. For some reason it made her crave the water. She dropped to her knees and spread out her shirt on an available patch of sand, pinned the opposing corners with her footwear, and from there, raced out into the lake.

For the remainder of the afternoon Erin alternated between swimming and that spot, sunbathing amidst the masses, feeling the usual weightlessness of the former, but surprising herself by the discovery of a similar euphoria back on shore. Bronzed by the better part of two weeks under the sun, the fine hairs on arms and stomach bleached to a fine white silk, she leaned back on her elbows and allowed herself to stretch her legs, point her toes out to the horizon with her knees locked straight. Feeling the flex in her thighs, and the lap of the water at her feet, she lay back, eyes wide to the clear sky above, opened her arms wide and drifted off to sleep.

~

But on this particular day, Megan's plans have been interrupted. As she strides towards the shore, lost in the comfort of her own company, she is stopped by Frannie Boisvert, pumping the pedals of her vintage bicycle, the front tire plowing sand at a comically slow speed. Meg braces herself for what she hopes will be nothing more than a cursory hello, but the rigid lines across the woman's weather-beaten forehead suggest this is just wishful thinking.

"There you are," she calls out, from still twenty feet away, before forgoing her brakes, opting instead to drop her heels to the ground in a less-than-graceful, yet effective, straddle-stop in front of the waitress. "Where are you headed?"

"Beach time."

"But the rally, Megan. Did you forget?" The woman checks her watch. "We're in front of the museum in an hour. Having you there would be a big advantage over town council."

Meg raises her head and smiles even as the pit of her stomach begins its familiar churn. She can feel her jaw tighten. Both responses are initiated to intercept the urge to scream something back in the candle shop owner's face, or just sprint off down the beach. Fight or flight, that's what these episodes of race and heritage had always occasioned, even during interactions with the so-called well-intentioned – the discussions with those *on her side* who, though usually careful never to say they *know how she feels*, are not above implying they seem to be championing *the cause* more acutely than she is. This they do by virtue of making public their activism. They march. They paint placards. They make speeches at rallies. In between these public demonstrations, they post on social media ... sharing and re-tweeting their battles and convictions. Meg glances up to find all of this present on Fannie's inquiring face. She has no doubt the woman's eyes are asking, *Why aren't you caring more about this? Why aren't you more involved?* And – most damningly – *Why don't you care as much as I do?* She has perceived the look – the questions – so many fucking times. And so many times she has wanted to step into the face of these well-intentioned people and scream, "Because you can leave it behind any time you want to ... like flipping your shoes off at the front door. You have that option!" Oh how she wishes she could make the sleepy majority feel the wariness that occurs whenever her skin tone, or hair, or heritage is singled out, even casually. The feeling of being instantly the *apart*. And whenever prejudicial comments are made in her midst, because someone has failed to *read the room*, to see that his or her audience is not the homogenous mass of white that is the norm for that person's universe, how she wishes they would understand her instinctive reaction is not first and foremost, anger or offence. It's fear. It's a fear that she has never been able to flee or confront. And without the fight-or-flight option at her disposal, she has always been left to swim in between, alone.

"What time do you want me there?" she hears herself sigh.

"Ah, that's more like it. The paper's coming at two."

~

~2~

The following day, however, was another matter. Though the weather was just as pristine, the sky as brightly azure, the rippled current just as genteel – she felt an ambiguity tempering its warmth from the moment she climbed out of the car.

Perhaps it had to do with her anticipating Meg's possible absence once again, then dealing with the doubt and the voices that this possibility engendered as it inched up on whatever resolve she had banked the previous afternoon. Rendering it disingenuous. Downgrading the day before to nothing more than a rationalization for hanging around the sand all on her own – a consolation prize that without any assurance of continuing a relationship with Meg, suddenly seemed such a shallow reward. Because, really, as her voices now shouted inside, what assurance did she have that anything with this woman would ever be experienced again?

She fought back with more rationalization. It was a Tuesday. Tuesday was the day of the week she and Meg had first spoken. So yes, while she had been counting on the idea that Tuesday afternoons were Meg's regular beach time, perhaps this particular Tuesday would not agree with her schedule. Perhaps work, or some other unexpected obligation, had come up, and that would be all there was to that. Nothing more to read into, should Erin not find any trace of her there ...

... which she did not. Not at their usual spot on the rocks, nor anywhere down the line of boulders, nor out on the breakwater, nor back around on the beach. And without the promise of Meg anywhere along the shoreline, all the sensations that had entertained her twenty-fours before were now also absent – replaced by the white noise of squawking gulls, and squealing children, the annoying obstacles of people and families spread-eagled across her pathway in the sand.

~

Ignatius Goyette

One further question. As barbecues are not an option, we are looking to do a picnic meal. Are there picnic tables available along the beach? If so, is it first come, first served?

Wendy Granger

A few at the south end that I can think of. One near the main parking lot if memory serves

Blanche King

Ignatius Goyette ... you'd be well advised to bring tables and chairs with you. As Wendy said, picnic tables are scarce and usually spoken for early in the a.m.

Ignatius Goyette

Blanche King ... *thank you for the information. We will plan accordingly, although it will be a tight fit in the minivan with my family, my mother and our two dogs*

Zack on the Six

Ignatius Goyette. Uh oh, you're gonna laugh.

Ignatius Goyette

??

Hank Lum

No dogs allowed on the beach May 24th
to Labour Day. Sorry, mate.

Blanche King

As if a dog being walked along a beach
makes more mess than these citiots
parked all day with their coolers and
loud speakers.

~

The plan for the following three days was to ignore the call of Lake Huron altogether, and instead give the reality of her life some much-needed attention. And what better way to do so than by getting a jump on setting up her classroom for September. Faithfully, she would drive only as far as Crestwood Elementary's parking lot. She would take out the storage bins with the classroom supplies and instructional posters, the accordion train banner with the alphabet spelled out in cursive, numeracy from one to ten, then by tens up to one hundred. She would open her files of autumnal pictures, depicting leaves of withered gold and blistered reds, lying as a blanket over dormant lawns, a cool sunlight filtering through naked lifeless tree branches. In a few short weeks, she would be hanging these images all over the walls, as she had every August for the past fifteen years. Then, all too soon, she would be replacing them with frigid shots of snow-drifted fields and frozen rivers. Then soon enough again, it would be spring's turn. It was all part of the bulletin-board rotation of seasons, complete with all the iconic decorations that each season brought along, cycled out one after another until the conclusion of another school year, when she would take them down and return them to their bins – so she would have somewhere from which to lift them out all over again.

Yes, she resolved to spend a few hours each of those three days, more if necessary, in the school until all her preparatory functions were complete, and everything was in place. Fuzzy-new tennis balls would be slit open and popped over the feet of the room's desks and chairs. The map of Canada would be traced onto the spare blackboard panel at the end of the room; the cut-outs of each province ready with sticky tack for kids to place. (The rudiments of the Canadian map were always her first social studies lesson of the fall.) The paint jars would be filled, the book corner spruced with a few new additions from the library, a few more from home. Rugs and throw pillows would be yanked from their garbage-bag repository in the utility closet, fluffed and aired out. Everything would be readied so that when that first bell rang – even if she were still at complete odds with these surroundings, still pining to feel the water flowing over her hips and shoulders as she dove into a wave – at the very least she would have the nuts and bolts of her profession in place to go through the motions of teaching a fresh batch of eight-year-old minds, moods and tantrums.

~

It would be some time well in the future – long after the very significant fall-out from her choices that summer had settled – when Erin would privately credit and blame, in equal measure, the sight of one particular fallen tree trunk in one of her classroom photos as the razor-edge of her point of no return. It was a maple toppled and cradled in the crook of another tree's branches, decaying just above a ground cover of frost. She would claim that it had suddenly chilled her to the bone. Left her in a sweat, with her arms and legs quivering, as if they were suddenly allergic to their surroundings, fevered by the confines of the four walls that had entrapped them. She would, at times, try to describe it as a *reaction.* Other times, like a seizure, or an attack. She would remember how she couldn't breathe. How she couldn't regulate her pulse. How the more she tried, the more her chest had tightened its grip around her, and the more she had panted helplessly for air.

~

At issue is the municipality's intent to dig away a portion of the sand dune next to the shore road and replace it with a concrete retaining wall. The stated rationale is safety. Town officials claim the area is overly congested with too many parked cars and too many pedestrians – specifically young children running for the beach – all too close to traffic. The shared belief of the factions opposed to the construction is that this is actually nothing more than a revenue grab to augment opportunities for paid parking. Collectively, they maintain that if public safety were actually the primary concern, other more effective and less intrusive solutions would be evident. Reduced speed limits, One-way traffic only. Converting the shore road into a pedestrians-only boulevard. The proof this isn't the case, they argue, is the fact that the council had approved these 'minor alterations' *in camera,* and with no public input or in fact notification until a week before tenders were secured.

The protesting factions represent a wide conflation of causes. Frannie is president of Pyette's Beach Heritage Association, representing, as far as Meg can tell, those mega-generation beach citizens who are all about maintaining the look and feel of the resort town as it appears in their collective rose-coloured memories. Anything mitigating that image, be it threats of box stores on the outskirts of town, fast-food franchises crowding out mom-and-pop restaurants, or the removal of the iconic sand-hills that grace the shoreline, and the Heritage Association will come calling.

So too might the Environmental Friends of Pyette, generally distinguishable from the Heritage contingent by their attire and accoutrements. There is an overall khaki theme to their look, from the buttoned shirts to the cargo shorts which are met at or near the knee with dark socks, and sensible hiking footwear. For a good number, Tilley hats and carbon-fibre walking sticks are also the order of the day, as are banners and signage with succinct but catchy phrases of protest. Meg is struck by their vitality – these are people who, on average, appear on in years, but nevertheless seem to sip from some bottomless well of enthusiasm.

As she approaches the rally, she passes one such woman talking into the phone of a cub reporter for the town's weekly paper. She speaks of the delicateness of the ecosystem, describing how erosion and wind would wreak havoc on the cut-away portions of beach dune, which would, in turn, jeopardize the nesting grounds of a number of species of shore birds that count on the unique habitat for their very survival. The cub nods dutifully, pushing his glasses back to the bridge of his nose at regular intervals – until he catches sight of the chief from the local band council. His attention now diverted, he strains to keep his phone recording in front of the environmentalist, while his eyes track the band leader's movements. Meg is curious to see what the woman's reaction will be to the sudden downgrade of attention. As she side-steps the interview, she peeks into the woman's face for any signs of micro-aggression – any pre-filtered look of disdain that might belie the amalgamation of interests currently united against their municipal government. Perhaps there's a slight pursing in the woman's lips. Maybe an exaggerated blink.

She inches her way towards the makeshift podium to hear the chief speak to the fact his band council was never notified of the town's plan to remove sections of the dune. The chief is clinical with his statements, explaining that federal and provincial governments are bound by law to undertake searches for possible First Nations land claims and title before commencing any public work project. And while municipal governments, because their resources are more limited, are not obligated to meet that high a threshold, he points out this is not an out for the town in this case, since Pyette Council is already currently in a legal dispute with his band over the very land where the retaining wall is to be erected.

A bit more of a crowd has now gathered, bringing Meg more uncomfortably into the midst of the proceedings. She shuffles backwards to return to the periphery, her attention shifting from the podium up to the facade of the building behind. *Pyette Beach Marine and Pioneer Museum* reads a sign spanning the length of the front verandah. It had been a fishing station once upon a time, or so she had once heard from one of her 11:00 a.m. coffee drinkers. Sometime in the 1860s, he had surmised. From there, it had transitioned into a hotel, after the lake had been fished out. Then it had been a small dance pavilion in the 1920s, and years after that some investors from the city had thrown money at its crumbling bones to try a fine-dining restaurant in the late 1980s. Then, ten years ago or so, the town purchased the property and renovated it back close to its original appearance, so it could house artifacts and memorabilia from *the town's origins*, as the sign's sub-caption put it.

Megan has never set foot inside. Has never once felt any compulsion to check the place out. Furthermore, until this very afternoon she has never bothered to ask herself why. Prior to her attendance today, she would have probably reckoned that, like a number of establishments around town – the Legion, the curling rink – it just wasn't her thing. But standing there taking in the museum's signage, a deeper motivation emerges. She wonders what time frame the museum has used for their particular notion of *origins*. Because she has her suspicions. She well imagines there is display after display that pays homage to schooners under sail blowing in from the open waters that were once teeming with trout and whitefish. Other rooms dedicated whole-heartedly to the mighty timber trade. Likewise considerable square footage reserved for the pioneer families who *cleared* the area. *Their* home in native land – start calibrations here.

And now here she was, being asked – it would seem – to represent her native heritage on behalf of those settlers' lineage, when she had no assurance there was anything inside the walls of the building hosting this rally that paid much homage to said ancestry. Oh sure, there would be something cursory. A lonely paragraph or two maybe ... on a foyer plaque? A broad-stroke or two for the centuries of heritage from the last ice age up to European arrival? *Pre-history* she remembers her high school history teacher calling it. History that hadn't grown up yet, presumably. Immature. Unsophisticated. But if a few meagre sentences was all she could hope for, then why was she needed here now? What weight could possibly be given to anything she has to say? What sincere interest would any of these well-intentioned people have in hearing the nuances of her own personal views? Her own opinions? Her individuality?

"I don't know what to make of this."

Meg turns to see that an East Indian man has slid in to listen beside her. He's older, with a relaxed paunch and a grey-speckled beard.

"It's a protest over removal of some of the dunes from–"

"Oh I'm aware of that," he cuts in. "I just mean the scene as a whole, you know?"

She likes the lilt of his accent, but feels it isn't appropriate to mention, so instead asks him for clarification. "So I'm a newer cottage owner," he explains. "But I made the mistake of joining the Friends of Pyette Facebook page. I gather a lot of the Heritage people on that site are here today. I read quite a bit of discussion every day about everything that's gone wrong with the beach. How much better it used to be. Too many tourists, too many vacationers. Too much change. It makes someone in my position a little nervous. Difficult to know where to go stand. Like I said, I'm a resident too, but to meet me walking down the beach ... what do these Heritage people see?"

"Most would let you be, wouldn't they?"

The man shrugs. "Publicly yes. If it's me alone. But what if it's my wife and kids? What if my brother and his family join us? How many people can I add before we are on the wrong side of that 'remember how great the beach used to be?' equation. How many people can I add before their anxieties kick in? Because, forgive me for saying this, but everybody has a number, if you know what I mean."

She's reasonably certain she does. Part of her, in fact, can't help wondering whether he would have dared initiate the same conversation if she had blond hair and blue eyes.

"Frannie there's alright though."

"You know her?"

"We have chatted a few times. She stopped me on the street last week to invite me here, although I believe she thought I was the fellow who runs the curry truck up past the marina. She asked me how the food business was going. I'm a retired dentist."

Megan nods, but can think of nothing to add.

"You know, I was in the Yucatan back ten years or so. A college buddy and I took the local bus from Cancun inland to Chichen Itza to see the Mayan ruins. We figured out it was literally a tenth the price of one of the tour buses from our hotel. Slower though. Lots of stops along the way. And it was crowded full, especially on the way back. Many local people going to look for work at the resorts. We sat beside one – a young mum with an infant in her arms. She was bottle-feeding the child with

Coca-Cola."

"Coke to a baby? Really?"

The man nods and wags a finger. "My friend had the same reaction. So much so, the next time we got together back home, the dinner party conversation was all about how Mexican mothers rot their children's teeth by feeding them soft drinks. Nothing about the young boys getting on to sell us slices of orange. Nothing about the tidy thatched homes along the roadside where these people lived and farmed. So clean and well-maintained with proud women leaning on their brooms and waving us by."

He glances over and notices Meg's subdued expression. "I'm sorry, I don't know why I'm rambling on about all of this, when we should be helping these people save their sand dunes." He checks his watch. "Then again, I should be getting home." A grin passes across his face. "But I will be careful not to be too conspicuous ... anything untoward just might get blamed on Sri Lanka as a whole, yes?"

Meg watches the man stroll off, back out the museum driveway and onto the shore road, hands in the pockets of his shorts, his flip-flops slapping at his heels. For some reason his absence gives her a sudden sensation of loneliness. She tries to ignore the feeling. For another few minutes she refocuses on the speeches, and the calls for action. But it's borrowed time. She wants to put this apprehension behind her – trade isolation for solitude. Quietly she backs out of the crowd, then breaks into a run as she heads for the water, passing the dentist with a wave of her hand.

~3~

Erin drove directly from school, changing in the beachside rest room. Immediately, she began swimming the length of the breakwater over and over, as though making up for lost time. She concentrated on everything Leyla had drilled into her years before. Arms reaching ahead at shoulder width, elbow bent with each turnover. Head down, not forward. Each stroke finishing long and through to the hip. After half an hour, with her stamina waning, she flipped her feet to the bottom in neck-deep water, blew a large measure of air from her lungs and waded back to shore. She gathered her towel and T-shirt to her chest, slipped her toes into her flip-flops and headed for the flat top of her favourite rock.

She pulled on her tee and sat down, drew up her knees to her chest, resting her head on her forearms. As it had a few days before, the gentle cadence of the lapping water mixed with the ambient noises of vacationers, with the distant but fervent cries of seagulls, and even further, the tinging of rigging against mast from a bell-choir of moored sailboats across the way in the marina. The sunlight sizzling on the water made slits of her eyes, which, combined with the lilting breeze, threatened to lull her bobbing head into full sleep right when Meg's distinctive laugh reached her ears.

It had company. Erin could pick out at least two other voices – men's voices – coming faintly from the other side of the breakwater. At first she cocked her head away from the wind to hear better, but to no avail, so tentatively she climbed up over the rocks. There she caught sight of Meg with three men actually, all with backs turned to her, walking towards the beach. She was quite certain that once again, two of them were the twenty-somethings she herself had encountered on her first visit to the lake.

They were chatting energetically. Meg's voice was animated

as she recounted a story with which Erin had no familiarity. Something about working in a restaurant. Waitressing and bartending. About the great tips one could pull in. The others chimed in too. The tallest of the three – blue shorts man – piped up that he had put himself through law school mixing drinks at a sports bar. Made most of his earnings via tips from middle-aged women while their husbands' eyes were glued to a football game.

"Down, boy," Meg chirped, as her hand fell loosely on his shoulder. Much of the ensuing conversation was too far away to be discernible. Nevertheless Erin continued monitoring their path until they reached the sand, where they threw down their belongings and, one by one, raced into the water, splashing one another with shouts of laughter. Now left with only body language as her guide – and, of course, whatever innuendo the voice in her head could apply to it – she watched Meg float on her back, making a large arc around her friends, rolling over and ducking below the surface, streamlined as ever, leaving little more than a ripple behind, until she cut the water open once more, coming up for air directly behind one of the others. The law-school grad again, Erin noted. She watched as Meg cupped a handful of water and poured it over the man's head, causing him to jump, then playfully grab her by the wrists and push her back into the surf, splashing her face and hair mercilessly with worked-up froth until the other two joined in, first allying with him, then turning on one another. Eventually the water games mellowed into independent swimming and diving, with the occasional exchange of conversation. After another thirty minutes – *God, have you been staring at them for half an hour?* – they all returned to stretch out on the sand. More indecipherable chatting followed, with heads turned sideways and hands shielding the glare of the sun. Once again there was some incidental touching – the brush of a hand against an arm or shoulder. Was it always initiated by Meg? It did seem that way from Erin's vantage point.

She shook her head and retreated back to her rock. Grabbed her sandals, slapping the soles together to rid them of grit that wasn't actually there. Tried desperately to tell herself this was none of her business, and that she didn't really want to see or know any more. *Oh, of course you do. That's all you want right now.*

She felt completely embarrassed. Then she felt doubly embarrassed for being reduced to feeling this way. After all, someone her age, with her ... *Your what? Life experience? Are you kidding? How about your marriage? Remember that? ...* She dropped the shoes. Made a fist and beat her hip with it. Then rubbed her palms vigorously, deciding then and there that it was time to come to her senses. That this obsession – this sun-drenched fog that had enveloped her for the past two weeks – had to end. That it was – in point of fact – already finished. *Assuming you can finish something that was never really anything in the first place.* Christ how she hated that voice – even as she nodded in agreement.

Making a concerted effort not to look in Meg's direction, she re-gathered her belongings, fished her keys from her towel roll and ran for the car.

~

But every few months she escapes, leaving her shoreline home for a weekend in the city. Toronto. Down Highway 410 to the 401, then past the airport. Beneath the wings of world travellers and jet-setters soaring above the commuter bustle of so many. With cursory looks sideways to the other lanes – the other drivers – she already feels the sharp thrill of anonymity. As always, she people-watches in order to decipher who is heading home, who is going out. But mostly she is searching for that fleeting eye contact with someone else showing a similar level of anticipation. Someone who, like herself, has the stereo flung to full volume and, if not singing along, is at least nodding to a beat, perhaps using the steering wheel as their own makeshift drum kit.

She will leave the car at a friend's place in the Annex, where she will be crashing afterwards. Maybe. A few years before, when a visit from Megan was still something to look forward to, the friend in question might have cleared his schedule, and altered his plans to coincide with hers. But that ship has long since sailed. Now it's mutually understood she is just looking for a place from which to launch her night out. Upon remembering the last few visits, he has cut her a duplicate key for the apartment. It's for the best. She tends to be out until 4 in the morning, and he is no longer invested in waiting up for her.

A change into her 'dancing dress' and she's off in a cab heading downtown for her first stop. As she approaches, the thump of the bass from the PA hits her chest rapid-fire, and she feels her pulse race, as if trying to catch up to the music's relentless beat. The doorman knows her. He gives her hand a squeeze and waves her in. She takes a deep breath in the corridor before climbing the stairs and stepping into the hall. It's a cavernous space composed mostly of light-beam and shadow. That's the appeal. Darkness punctuated only by intermittent columns of red, blue and green, all doing zig-zag patterns across a sea of bodies moving like a current. At the far end of the club, hoisted on risers, is the house DJ, the only fully illuminated person in the entire room. With headset mic strapped on, the woman moves with the beat enticing the room to do likewise.

At the near corner Meg spots Matt behind the bar. She wonders if he remembers chatting with her – shouting into each others' ear lobes actually – the last time she was here. They had tried to carry on a conversation about the beach. He had spent some weekends there as a kid, at least that's what she thought he was telling her. It was sporadic. He was busy. She was dancing. And it had been loud, as it is now again.

She glides out onto the floor, her stride slowly morphing into movement that is neither choreographed nor known. She will simply move as her body dictates, as if there is a private breeze buffeting her with a rhythm accessible only to her and whoever dares to join her – whoever catches her eye or leans in, or moves against the fabric of her dress. And if unwanted hands reach too far, if open palms start to close around a hip or breast, she merely dances away, sometimes pausing just long enough to place a 'no thanks' into the ear of the offender, possibly even accompanied by a peck on the cheek. This is her go-to tactic – eluding bees with honey.

~

"Hey, wait up!"

In a few loping strides Meg reached her, turned her around by the shoulders. But Erin broke free and kept walking. Hugging her shirt and shoes to her chest, she squeezed her eyes shut to keep down the welling she could feel about to emerge. Meg took two more quick steps to get ahead of her, this time blocking her path with a hand on each arm. "Hey, what is it?"

"It's nothing … nothing." Erin's voice was barely a whisper.

"It's not nothing. You're upset. How long have you been here?"

She shrugged, then slapped her arms to her sides. "Four days," she blurted out. "Four days I've been out here trying to find you. Sitting here pretending everything was all ... cool." She waved her sandals towards the rocks.

"Look, I'm sorry, but I've been busy–"

"Oh I can see you're busy."

Instantly, the hands cradling Erin's elbows released, rising in tandem with palms held outward. Meg set her jaw and nodded. "Okay ... well... yeah, see you around."

"No ... no. I'm sorry." It was Erin's turn to chase and circle. "It's me, alright? I'm mad at myself. For thinking we ..." her words trailed off again under the growing breeze, and she could only complete the apology with another shrug. She felt small – felt far below her actual height; far beneath the lanky confidence of the woman she'd had under surveillance all afternoon.

A gust of wind picked up Meg's bangs, which she shook from her face. Her hands were now making a statement on her hips, her eyes running the length of the horizon south to north and back again. And just as Erin, fearing the worst, felt her own feet twitching to escape the irreparable awkwardness – *of your own design, I might add* – she actually thought she detected the flash of a grin cross Meg's face. A glimmer of a reprieve. The hope was confirmed when Meg bit at her lip and looked back amused.

"So you were jealous," she said very quietly.

"No, it's not that–"

"You saw me with those guys in the water and you got mad." She took a step forward and ran her hand down Erin's arm until their fingers intertwined, then sang "You got jealous" twice softly in her ear, and would have continued longer had the school teacher not pulled her close with an unexpected and lingering kiss.

"Holy shit," Meg said when they finally broke for air, foreheads still leaning against one another. Erin was breathing hard. Her eyes were back down on the ground. She became aware of voices. A series of whoops from somewhere out on the breakwater. Men's voices. Boys' too. With frat-like yips and howls of approval. She braced herself to look up, envisioning a line of them with beer-can salutes or, worse yet, with phones aloft at the end of outstretched arms. She felt dizzy. She felt both reborn and too old. More alive and more scared than she could ever remember being. Another set of catcalls and her shoulders tightened, her arms automatically retracting over her chest.

"Ignore it," Meg whispered, stepping even closer and putting her arms around the small of Erin's back. But then, in the very next instant, she jumped back, rubbed her face vigorously with an open palm. "Holy shit, lady," she repeated. "That tongue of yours ..." She kicked the sand, and stepped in a tight circle, finishing up right back in front of Erin's face. "I mean, you got more balls than ... well, all those guys and their balls!"

Meg stepped closer again, taking both hands from down at her sides. "And just so you know," she whispered, "I get my weed and edibles from those guys, that's all. I know ... there's a dispensary up by the strip mall, but what can I say? Old habits die hard, I guess. Besides, those guys always have product on them and I know I can get a deal."

She returned a kiss – shorter and gentler this time. One for which Erin decided to leave her eyes open, to take in this woman delivering her affection, only to find Meg was watching her too. Meg pulled on her arm. "Come on," she said dragging Erin back out to their rocks and all but tackling her into the water.

Had the teacher's inner voice – the voice that lived to doubt – still been fully engaged it may have won a battle, noting this was Meg's second emotional retreat in a matter of seconds. Her second vacillation between tenderness and ... and what? Whimsy? Playfulness? Unpredictability? *And has she not come across that way on each of your other visits? A bit elusive, a bit unpredictable. Almost as if it were maybe even by design? Something that worked for her? A safety measure? An upper hand?* The voice would have its say in good time. It always did. But for the moment it was lost as they swam semi-interlocked, floating around to the far side of a few of the larger boulders that formed a small alcove of chest-deep water, out of sight and earshot of passers-by, taking turns wrapping their legs around each other, leaning back to float with arms relaxed across the water. They splashed each other's faces, stroked each other's backs. Kissed every so often ... each time a little longer, a little deeper. Then, once out in deeper water, they reached for the tie at one another's top. Then hip.

~

She would spend the first five miles of the trip home singing along to the radio, at one point valiantly trying to administer a high harmony to the Tragically Hip song that had serendipitously come across the airwaves – an occurrence that, in her blissful state, she took as a sign. She shook out her hair and let it blow as it wished, twisted her scrunchy around her wrist. Let the coolness of the breeze refresh her baked forehead, her arms, the tops of her thighs. When subsequent songs failed to live up to her sudden fondness for Gordon Downie's singular voice, she occupied herself with the passing fields, the rows of maple and oak that lined the county road. For so much of her life these images had been a source of comfort. Serenity even. From the verdant panorama of rolling crops to orchards cuddled around red and yellow brick farmhouses, the most stately sporting expansive crew-cut lawns bordered by freshly painted fences – these vistas had once been such reliable friends. The same could be said for the serene interruptions of forest stands, and the gently flowing rivers and creeks that happened by. There was a time all of it was more than sufficient to serve as the extent of her universe. From her days away, first as an undergrad at a campus a mere two hours south, then teachers' college in Kingston, her regularly scheduled trips home had marked her days. They had been, in point of fact, her salvation from the necessity of leaving her parochial upbringing. Each trip home had been clockwork-scheduled for every second weekend – be it by bus or a shared ride with another student with similar sensibilities, also hedging their bets as they vainly tried to hang onto their childhood. Vainly tried to keep their past and their future heaped onto the present.

Erin had often made these trips with her head pressed against the car window, peering up at the trees flashing past ... endeavouring to take them in as though seeing them for the very first time. During her undergrad years such moments had begun as soon as she left the city's limits, as street lights and commuter traffic slowly gave way to the flat open landscape of Ontario farmland. In teachers' college the wait had been a little longer ... until she was past Greater Toronto and had turned north to leave the four-lane thoroughfares in the rearview mirror. Then her senses would awaken and she would drink in the colour of the foliage in October, or the stark barren branches of November, the measure of snowbank against tree trunk in winter, the decline of those levels as spring began its thaw. She had needed each and every season to get her through those years. To get by. To manage the business of growing up and leaving home. To know that – if nothing else – she could always come back here, not just momentarily, but someday, for good ... reunited with the comforts of her very specific *environment* once more. In the back of her mind, that had always been the goal. So when a full-time teaching position came up in the very county of her birth, she jumped at the opportunity.

But now ... now she was left to wonder how it could have taken over twenty years – a marriage, a career, and raising a daughter – before the question of *Is that it?* reared its disruptive voice. It hit her full force halfway home – about the third song after The Hip – leaving her nothing less than completely astonished by how little she recognized the sensibilities of the young woman she had once been. For here she was, soaring down the road, hair flying around, still in her two-piece, still tingling from the beach behind her, realizing that she was now, in fact, distinctly at odds with her former self, likewise with the landscape around her. There was a restriction to the canopy of limbs overhanging the road – a weight to the late afternoon shadows it cast. There was a sense of entrapment and an unforeseen anxiety of feeling confined. Hemmed in where she no longer wished to be. Landlocked. She felt the same feeling of panic starting to surface that had befallen her in her classroom that morning. And in that instant, all the excitement of having been with Meg was suddenly replaced by the fear of missing out on even one more day with her. It was an unmistakable shift that manifested itself with the restless realization that the sun on her shoulders and the warm grit of the sand clinging to her calves were destined to be but a brief and fleeting experience. The feeling would hang over her the rest of the way home. There it would remain as she cooked a light dinner (barbecued salmon fillets served with rice and grilled peppers, as was their Fridays). And it would still be present as she scrubbed the grill and rinsed the plates. Still there as she stared into the TV screen at a home renovation show, while he retreated to his home studio (as was every evening). Indeed it would still cling to her hours later as she aimed the pedestal fan across the sheets and climbed into bed beside his sleeping form, his arms thrown over his head, mouth open and snoring. When she would reach to turn off the bedside light and then, under the cloak of darkness, begin caressing her thigh.

~

They ended up stretched out on their stomachs across their boulder, both propped up on their elbows, face to face.

"You know, I probably wouldn't have talked to you in the first place if I wasn't a little bit buzzed." Meg played with the hairs on Erin's forearm, awaiting a reaction to the admission. "You've never tried it, have you?"

The school teacher shook her head and sighed. "Nope. I attacked you stone sober," she replied with a grin. She rested her head on her forearms. "Keep doing that."

Meg laughed, crossed her ankles and kicked her feet up in the air behind her as her fingers combed a slow figure eight. For the time being they both rested comfortably and silently, with the warmth of the sun radiating off their backs and the sounds of the beach-world at bay.

"So what all do you take?" Erin's voice emerged muffled out from under her armpit.

"Mostly edibles. Like I said, those guys always have a supply on them. Chewy little bites of splendour," she sighed and flipped over on her back, momentarily forgetting she was topless before grabbing Erin's shirt to drape over her, her eyes squinted shut against the sun. “You should try some. I mean, I guess there’s still a stigma with some people but there shouldn’t be, right? It’s completely legal and anybody not using it for a little hit is using it for arthritis, or cancer, or chronic fatigue, so ...”

“Would I like it?”

Meg jumped to her knees, threw on the top and reached for the pocket of her shorts. She took out what looked to Erin like a flattened gummi bear, or one of the gelatinous wads of something-or-other she occasionally scraped from the underside of a classroom desk.

“Just take this tiny little bit. On your tongue.”

“Do I chew?”

“If you want, or let it dissolve.”

Erin pressed the candy between her tongue and the roof of her mouth, her eyes dancing up at Meg, who stared back with a curious grin.

“So you’ve really never–”

“Not even once,” Erin replied, rolling onto her back. By way of preparation she closed her eyes and folded her hands across her chest to brace herself for – or against – whatever was about to ensue. Meg picked up one of her hands and latticed their fingers together (actually playing with Erin’s wedding band absently for a moment) while she monitored Erin’s nervous eyes rapidly darting back and forth. She pressed a hand to her patient’s chest. “You’re fine, you’re fine,” she assured her, even as a slightly panicky voice from high in the rafters of the teacher’s thoughts fought back. *This isn’t you.*

“I don’t feel anything yet. ”

“You won’t. It’s very gradual.”

Meg lay back down diagonally to her, using Erin’s thigh as a pillow. She lowered her sunglasses from her forehead to await the bliss from the portion she had reserved for herself. They drifted in and out of light sleep for the better part of an hour until, slowly but steadfastly, the warm gentle sound of the breeze and lapping shore was infiltrated by bright metallic patterns strung across the otherwise dark canvas of Erin's closed eyes. With them came a growing awareness of more distant clamour – boat engines, swimmers somewhere out beyond them. Punctuating her sound-strings were components of colour splashing across the inside of her eyelids ... first orange, then yellow and greenish blue ... a constant shifting between them, moving and fading, too elusive to capture in any sort of sequence.

"What?" she blurted out, suddenly aware that someone was leaning against her. She blinked her eyes open to find Meg trembling in silent laughter.

"It's okay." She reached out and caressed Erin's ankle. Instantly the string-patterns returned. For one thick moment – an eternity of an instant – a blanket of warm shivers engulfed her. It was nothing but pleasure in the form of waves and vibrations and the soft hand of her friend.

The voice within tried interrupting again – tried to snip the thread of the euphoria. To disconnect the bliss by severing the connective tissue of her colours and sounds. It was a counter-attack in the form of an observation, insidiously aimed to plant a seed of impermanence on the moment. Like picking a child's birthday party as the moment to inform them of their inevitable mortality. Yes, she had loved, absolutely loved the way Meg was assuring her and tending to her – the way she lay her hand to Erin's breast, stroked her leg. But at the same time, Meg still did not use her name. She had not once said, "I've got you, *Erin.*" In fact, other than the one occasion early on, Meg never used her name *at all. Did she even remember it? Are you really anything more than an afternoon hook-up?* In that moment, Erin's breath was caught short, lost in unanticipated suspicion. But then, an instant later, came the inverse, and another shimmer of uncharted pleasure washed over her, which she soaked in, once again aware of nothing but the colourful motion of her sensations.

"How is it now?" Meg called from under her sunglasses, reaching blindly again for Erin, this time patting her stomach.

"I want to swim," Erin replied.

"What? No, later. You should just chill."

"No, I wanna swim. I hear music in my head and I wanna swim to it."

Meg flipped back onto her stomach and tossed her glasses back into her hair, a big smile beaming across her face. "Oh you are definitely into it, sister."

Quickly Erin sat up and slipped off their rock into the cool water, feathering her hands across the surface. It was The Hip she was hearing, she was pretty sure. Her head began to bob with the rhythm of her private soundtrack. The notes growled with a sharp edge, an emotionally cacophonic precision, that washed by and circled back, fading and then surging again, like ripples returning to their splash. And there was a thickness to the melody, wherever it was coming from (which seemed like everywhere). She felt like a blind man just learning to see.

So this is what Trevor had always been on about, all those times in college, when she had stayed home in her room curled up with a 'sweater novel', in the company of some middle-aged introvert's musings. All of those house parties ... all those dorm floor blowouts ... beer pong tourneys, the games of mushroom roulette that she – if she put in any appearance at all – had merely endured, tethered as she was to her one-beer maximum, and resolutely fused to a chair or sofa near the exit, feet firmly on the floor, away from the slippery spills on any unscripted influences.

She would call him right away, she decided then and there. She would tell him today that she had finally experienced what he had for years embraced. And she would thank him too ... for having the insight to know that he could have never pushed this experience on her. She would confide that she had always appreciated the way he slipped away from her presence when partaking, and that she knew he had done so out of the need to spare her the effort of reconciling his penchant for the stuff with their upbringing – an upbringing which had unquestioningly and thoroughly damned recreational drug use of any description. She would tell him she understood he had managed things that way so he could keep the differences between them from becoming obstacles ... so they could stay included in each others' lives.

"Like a lover who doesn't know your name," she blurted out suddenly into the here-and-now, almost singing the words.

"What was that?" Meg called back, tying off her top and slipping into the water as well. Erin waded awkwardly back towards her.

"I think I always wanted music to be my drug," she announced, considerably louder than she had intended, the hint of melody still in her voice. Then she decreed she had changed her mind and she wanted to sunbathe some more. She pulled Meg back out of the water and lay back on her stomach, this time discarding her towel in favour of the heat from the stone against her stomach and thighs.

"Unclip me. I want some more colour there," she said, and Meg obliged, following it up with some sunscreen massaged into her back and shoulders.

"Did you know I was a music major for a while in college?" she mumbled, then wagged a finger in the air above her head. "No, of course you don't because we weren't allowed to say anything about that ..." She plopped her face down on her arms. "I thought I wanted to *study* music, you know? But I think what I really wanted ... was *this*."

"And what is *this* exactly?"

Erin rolled over topless and pulled her friend down to her. "*This*," she whispered to her ear and laughed. "Because, you know what? A music degree is just the steroid version of getting the gold star at the top of your homework. Credentials and resumé fluff. Well-rounded person, job-interview filler, qualified-to-look-after-other-people's-children-so-they-can-grow-up-pleading-for-gold-stars-too shit. But ... here's the thing!" She drew her lips up against Meg's ear lobe and whispered. "*That's not music*."

Meg lifted herself up, draped an arm to cover Erin's breasts and stared amused into her wide-open eyes.

"Man, you are flying."

~4~

The residue of the day, the grit of wind-assisted granules that had once strictly been the domain of her rocks and shoreline, she could now feel around her ankles, beneath the bed sheet, as she rubbed her feet together, scouring the image she had of herself – and that she knew others held for her. Steady and sensible. An inch away her husband's inert form slept on, as still as furniture, sturdy and lifeless. A man who asked so very little of her, he had grown seemingly content to leave more and more of himself on the edit room floor of her life, with barely a scene or speaking part shared between them. And yet there he still was, not a breath away from her body and skin. The skin *she* had touched not hours before. Touched, caressed and awakened from a long winter's nap.

Unable to sleep Erin did what she had begun doing for the past week's worth of stiflingly restless nights. She slipped out from under the covers and up past the low hum of the oscillating fan aimed at their headboard. Silently she grabbed her laptop, and escaped to the back porch to curl up in the wicker chaise, fingers poised at the ready over the keyboard.

~

Sometimes however, the hands are welcome. Sometimes they are the desired response to her own instigation. Her last time down, even though Matt had caught her eye (and she was quite certain it was reciprocated), the night had ended with the twenty-something student from Centennial College – she of the flowing bohemian hair and flowing voile skirt. They had adjourned to her loft in the east end via a rather passionate Uber ride.

Having such youthful eagerness returned always proves such an intoxicating force. That and her delicious anonymity. She can be anyone she wants, on these nights in the shadows. That is the reason for these sojourns after all, is it not? To lose her *self* completely in the soup of rhythms and beats and bodies. Or is it actually a matter of *finding* her self? She has never been able to decide, but for the duration of her nights out at least, the lack of an answer does not bother her. Because in the end, the allure of surrendering to the pounding speakers and strobe lighting means not having to stop and parse out such distinctions. The allure is the effects of a half-dozen Manhattans, or the hits from a communal bong on the rooftop patio, or shared joints while lying on the futon of a 21-year-old, third-year theatre major from Orangeville who kept on shushing Meg's orgasms for fear of awakening her Jehovah's Witness room-mate.

Distinctions are for the morning after. Often early in the pre-dawn glimmer of daylight, interrupting her own private afterglow as she safely makes her way back to her friend's accommodation. It is then she needs to reaffirm that these weekends away are solely about the flame of momentary tenderness – the intimate connections of beautifully random souls. It's then she reminds herself the goal is to explore, but not conquer. To explore and to share in as many experiences as possible. Not everybody's cup of tea, her libertine ways, she fully understands. But for her, it feels pure and natural, and beautifully temporary. Pure and natural *because* it is temporary, she clarifies – right before the more mundane contingencies of the coming day interrupt her testament.

On this occasion with the muscle memory of a man named Evan – his broad shoulders overtop of her, sliding back and forth through her palms – that interruption is in the form of a plan for once she's back in Pyette. She will drop her luggage at the apartment and maybe grab a shower. Definitely change her clothes. Then she will head over to her mother's house and pick up Kyle, hoping against hope that he has slept for his grandma this time.

Chapter Four

~1~

The following afternoon was a shopping day for Leyla. Erin calculated that if she picked her mother-in-law up before noon, she'd still have time to make it out to the lake for a quick swim.

All morning long the radio had been promising a storm front, set to sweep in over Lake Huron sometime in the late afternoon or early evening. Forecasts were modelling a fairly severe break to the weeks of pressure that had been building, soaking up every last bit of humidity before it uncoiled like a spring. But by mid-morning there was no indication that such climatic drama would actually unfold. The sun continued to pound down as it had for days on end, baking lawns and scorching gardens. There was no change at noon either, when Erin ushered the shuffling feet of her mother-in-law towards the sliding doors of the Shoppers Drug Mart. One step inside and the store's air conditioning hit the school teacher like a glacier, putting Erin to work rubbing the goosebumps from her arms and shoulders. Leyla, on the other hand, demonstrated no reaction. Instead she commenced with her routine, which always began by insisting on the full-size cart, not a basket, even though her shopping list was but a half-dozen items – and a list that Erin had committed to memory for the better part of a decade. They would inch their way past the opening kiosks – counters rife with powerful scents and bold make-up choices – before stopping to mull over the infinity of toothpastes, with their infinity of flavours and promises. Then it would be the toothbrushes where, as often as not, Leyla would pick out a soft-bristled design, usually in a blue, toss it in her cart with a shrug, or an "Oh I don't know anymore" before doubling back and blindly grabbing the nearest tube of paste to fire in on top. She would then inspect but not purchase any combination of deodorants, bandages and liniments, as she struggled to remember which aisle was home to the incontinence pads. Aisle four Erin could have told her, if such direction was actually invited. But it was not. Not any longer. The unspoken rule now was that once Leyla had spotted her *private things*, Erin was sent to grab a bag of chocolate chip cookies from the confectionery aisle. "The chewy kind, not the hard ones," her mother-in-law would advise, willingly citing aloud her ever-loosening dentures as rationale, for all to hear. Upon her return Erin would glance to see the pads already tucked away in a white plastic bag that had been brought from home. It saddened her, this latent shame that had invaded the woman's twilight years. This was, after all, the same person who used to take her and Avery to the bay so many summers ago, strip to her underwear and jump in the water without a moment's thought or concern for any bystanders' sensibilities.

Leyla followed Erin's eyes down to the cart. "So ... I suppose you're still spending all your time trying to be a writer?" It was said in a tone that she had rarely heard from the woman's lips – and never about this. There was, to Erin's ear, a clear implication that her writing was nothing more than folly, a less-than-veiled suggestion that this habit of hers was a luxury that came at the expense of tending to her real duties. Her marriage ... *making* the home. It left Erin momentarily reeling over the possibility that the comment was actually not a one-off, but a tip-of-the-iceberg sentiment that Leyla had been suppressing for God knows how long. (Pent up like a storm front poised to explode – if Erin allowed herself the use of such an obvious metaphor.)

She expected this kind of skepticism from others. Audrey, for one. And her own mother – well, that was a given. But from Ross's mum? It seemed so totally against form. She had always assumed her mother-in-law was nothing but empathetic. She had always assumed Leyla understood that this interest in writing was never a matter of luxury, but of refuge. Something to help get through life

... life with *her* son. (Speaking of frivolous hobbies ...) Christ, on troublesome days – those deathly silent non-communicative *wed-locked* days – it was the only redemption. What had begun as random thoughts, scribbled ad hoc in a notebook here and a journal there, had grown into a regimen – and a rather prolific regimen at that, especially once Ross started throwing every minute of his own free time into his own stockpile of never-ending obsessions. But even if Leyla did harbour secret misgivings about Erin's creative outlet, even if she wasn't actually the ally her daughter-in-law had always assumed she was, so what? Erin quickly reminded herself that she still had her writing group – still had at least the makings of a network of like-minded souls who saw the value of honing their thoughts and feelings via the written word. And even if that weren't the case – again – did it really matter? Even if her musings were only ever destined to remain locked safely in a basement filing cabinet, could she still not enjoy the enterprise for its own sake? Who would care if the fruits of her literary labours never reached another set of eyes?

Well, maybe if those eyes were Meg's. The voice had come out of the blue, dangling the notion before her so quickly that, for just a second, she was lost, daydreaming the possibility of being for Meg what her favourite writers were for her. Munro, Shields, Urquhart, Hay ...

"Aaaah!"

Erin's head snapped up to find Leyla back down the aisle staring into space in front a wall of household cleaning products. "Is this one of those ...?" She waved a small can of kitchen cleanser in the air as she tried to complete the question. "Those ... oh damn it, spit it out, woman," she snapped and fired the product to the floor.

"It's for counters and sinks," Erin replied, bending down to pick up the can. "Did you want–"

"No, no, no!"

"So you don't want–"

"The words, child," she blurted, shaking her fists in the air, her cane dropping to the floor, which Erin retrieved as well. "What I want are the words ... but they just don't ..."

Erin swept in to take her by the elbow. "It's okay, it's okay. How about we take a minute and sit? I'm sure there's a chair at the back."

"Talcum! Christ almighty, there it is – finally. I need talcum."

"Well I can go find you some. Let me do that while you just rest here." Erin grabbed the chair from a clerk who had heard the commotion and come to the rescue. With a silent nod of thanks, she was about to dart quickly to the next aisle when her mother-in-law snatched her by the hem of her shorts, almost pulling her across her lap.

"I'm eighty-three!"

Erin gathered the woman's hands onto her lap and crouched low to look up from below her chin. "And you're doing so well. I only hope I'm half as–"

"Oh that's enough! ... I'm not fishing for glory. What I'm saying is I'm eighty-three and I don't want ..." Her voice trailed away and her chin began to tremble.

"Don't want what?"

"To be done, child ... I'm not ready to be through." She released the grip on Erin's clothing, began smoothing out the creases on her own slacks. "Don't you think I'd like to be able to do all this on my own? Not have to drag you around every other week?"

"But I've told you, it's no bother. I'm more than happy to–"

"Or come up with the name of something when I need to?" She tapped the heel of her hand against her forehead. "I swear I know the words are in there. I can feel them, you know? But somewhere between my head and sliding down to my jaw, they just get ... stuck

... or take a wrong turn, or ... something. Things I need. Names of people I've known my whole life ..." Leyla paused to straighten up on the chair, blew out a long sigh and pulled a slightly tired tissue from her cuff to daub at the corners of her mouth.

"I'm eighty-three years old and I still want it all to do." She shook her head and looked around the store. "Because mark my words, child, I'm here to tell you, it won't seem like a long time. I know it should. But it doesn't." She returned the Kleenex to her sleeve, then reached for the cane, setting her hands and chin on the handle. "I always thought there'd come a time when it would feel like I've done enough, but it turns out, no matter how many days and years you get ... you just want more ... even if it's just more of the same old thing. Toothbrushes. Cookies." She prodded at the unmarked plastic bag in the cart. "Surely you know what I'm talking about, yes? Even at your tender age?"

"Leyla, you do know I'm forty-four."

"Pretty tender from where I'm sitting, Missy." She poked her cane again, this time against her daughter-in-law's thigh. "Look at you with all your tanned arms and legs. Hair still long down your shoulders. Always dressed descent ... way past when I gave up trying, I'll tell you that much. Although to be fair, you haven't got it as bad as some."

She nodded back over her shoulder and Erin's gaze followed in the direction of a woman working at the fragrance counter who also appeared to be in her mid-forties. She was dressed in a jet-black blazer worn over a crisp, only fractionally buttoned, white blouse, and sported a level of make-up and mascara that Erin had to admit looked severe enough to limit facial expression.

Leyla waved a hand for assistance to get back to her feet. "Oh well, to each their own I guess," she mumbled. "Everybody deals with growing old their own way. My neighbour Claire is certain she can hear her dead father's voice when she's asleep ... thinks he's guiding her and whispering in her ear from the great beyond." She shook her head and scrunched up her bottom lip. "Nothing like that's ever happened to me, not even once," she said. "But I'll tell you what I have felt. I've felt my own father's chest at his funeral. That's right. I reached right down into that coffin and put my hand on him. Felt how cold and hard it was right below the surface. Like somebody had made a sculpture out of him and just wrapped it up in his skin to fool us. Which, in a sense, is exactly what they did, I suppose."

She pushed herself to her feet and started shuffling towards the cash registers. Erin watched her go, noting that the storm clouds that had so quickly gathered inside her had broken – at least partially. Most likely, it was the best possible outcome. Given her stage in life, she had probably learned to weather such depressions moment to moment. Perhaps she had even come to accept that some unresolved pressure would always remain hanging over her. Because she had reached the age when a return to clear skies was now always understood to be a temporary thing.

~2~

The idea struck Erin shortly after she dropped Leyla off and was back in her car on the edge of town heading for the beach. In retrospect – and there would be considerable retrospect – she would never find a valid justification for her decision beyond the vague association it had with the words of her mother-in-law still reverberating in her ears. *I still want it all to do.*

On an impulse she had yanked on the steering wheel and sped back into town – down the hill, a left and then another, to her house, where she raced inside straight down the steps to the far corner of the basement, opening the bottom drawer of an old solid oak filing cabinet that had come from the family store years before. She pulled out a small stack of papers and for a few seconds studied the top sheet with its title printed boldly across its width (her name, much smaller ... more of a whisper in a tiny font underneath). She was about to read on – flip to the next page and examine her work one last time. But Leyla's voice echoed once again, so without further deliberation she slipped the pages into a manila envelope and made for the car, lest she lose her built-up will.

~

By the time she made it out to Pyette Beach the sky had finally clouded over. Her tires spit gravel as she pulled up and parked. From the back seat, she grabbed an extra cover-up, the manila envelope, the thermos of coffee she had packed for the shopping trip but hadn't had time to get to. Her regular glasses, since the sun had vacated the day. Then her phone – for no specific reason. Had she been less rushed, she might have paused to consider the number of items which she suddenly had found the need to bring along. Furthermore she might have realized that this was in fact the first time – ironically now, since time was of the essence – that she had paused to pack. That on every other occasion she had actually done the exact opposite – stripped herself down to what, in the breathless calm of an endless August afternoon, had been an intoxicating simplicity. (*Alas, sensibilities can change, just like the weather.*)

She fired the items into a large straw tote that she found on the floor of the back seat – save the envelope, which she carefully slid down the side of the bag to protect from any unwanted folds and creases. Then it was off along the beach towards their spot, her eyes working to scan the thinning crowd, much of which was heading back towards her in the opposite direction. Given how the clouds were piling up to the west, only the heartiest were staying put. She noted three windsurfers in wetsuits revelling in the growing violence the lake had on offer, as they skipped and danced from crest to crest a hundred feet off shore. Likewise a couple was setting up a camera on a tripod, looking almost giddy as they aimed its lens directly toward the approaching chaos.

In a few minutes she was out by their rock. There she spotted Meg, sandals in hand, cover-up on, climbing back up from the water's edge. "No, don't go yet," Erin called out and broke into a jog to get there more quickly. Here again, had time been less precious, perhaps at that point she would have heard the unintended desperation in her voice. Perhaps too, she would have noticed from the cocked head and curious glance that Meg had also heard it.

"Everything alright?"

Erin took a moment to catch her breath, then reached out and pulled Meg in for a hug, a decision that instantly proved far more awkward than she had anticipated. "Sorry," she found herself mumbling, "I was just hoping to catch you before you ... I mean, I was hoping you'd be here."

Meg stared at her, which did nothing to preserve Erin's nerve.

"I was in for about a half-hour," she said finally, gesturing with her sandals out towards the darkened horizon. "If you want to go, you'd better hurry."

"No ... I mean, yes, I do. But what I was hoping ..."

The words were not flowing as she had rehearsed the whole drive out, and the reception she was receiving was not what she had envisioned. "Can we talk for a few minutes?"

"Well I'm actually late to–"

"It will only take a minute," Erin interrupted, and in doing so finally heard herself through Meg's ears. Heard the nervous flutter in her words that surely was the cause of Meg's hesitation. *Looks like somebody's awkward first impression finally decided to show up.*

"I'm sorry, but after we had our last few ..." Unable to label their encounters properly, Erin's voice trailed away leaving her merely to wave her satchel in the direction of the gathering swells. She could feel Meg's eyes bearing down on her. Maybe this was actually her true expression, her resting face when there was no sunshine to brighten it.

"Erin, what is it? What's wrong?"

She wanted to interpret the question as one of concern, but there was an impatience to Meg's voice. Moreover the hand placed on Erin's suddenly seemed patronizing and void of tenderness ... as though put there to subdue. Or sedate. Like an anesthetic.

"I wanted to give you this," Erin said finally, reaching into the tote bag and pulling out the manila envelope, just as the first drops of rain splat across her forearm. "It's for you ... it's ..." Again descriptions failed her. "I wrote this for you."

Meg stared at the envelope, then back at Erin. She opened the flap to peek down the length of its first page. "*Between the Sand and the Sea*," she read, then – for a moment at least – grinned. "Your last name is Leith." (Once more, with the luxury of time and consideration, Erin might have realized this too was something she had never packed for a day at the beach – her surname.)

Meg pulled the pages from their cover, and, despite the building frequency of raindrops, began flipping through them.

"No!" Erin blurted out, the plea in her voice catching Meg off guard yet again. "Not here."

"What's wrong with here?"

"I don't want to be here when you do."

"Well you can have your swim if you hurry. This doesn't look too long, and I'm a pretty quick reader."

Erin scanned the now mountainous cloud front. "No, I think I've left it too late," she said. "I'll be in my car. That's me over there," she said, pointing to the black Kia Soul, now one of the few remaining vehicles still parked beachside. "If you want to read through it now, I'll wait to see what you think." Then, without waiting for a response, she bolted for her car, groping back in her satchel for her keys. "I've never done anything like this before, by the way," she called back over her shoulder. At least that's what it would sound like to Meg. In truth, it was a bit difficult to make out definitively, for the first roll of distant thunder chose the very same moment to rattle across the horizon.

~

The humidity hangs over his van like a lead sheet. He had felt it building and pressing on his chest and labouring his breathing all afternoon. It was usually the case when the barometric pressure shifted into high gear. For some, it is the cause of migraines, or depression ... or a whole laundry list of climatic dis-ease. For him it starts and ends with the respiratory system.

His saving grace was always the storm front itself – the excitement of the most severe weather that summer could throw at him.

And sure enough, three or four times a year – if he was lucky – he would strap himself in the minivan, laptop beside him, open to a weather imaging app. He would race down the road leaving a plume of spray behind him, eyes constantly checking on the rolling cloud line – waiting to see if it was going to tumble forward on a horizontal axis. His phone would be out, his head set on, the Canada Warning number on speed-dial with one touch so he could 'ground truth' whatever Environment Canada was picking up via satellite. He would often be asked to differentiate the lightning he was seeing. They were always interested to know that ... whether it was sheet or staccato ... if it was cloud-to-air, or cloud-to-ground. And all the while he busied himself with these pursuits he would fail to notice his breathing had returned to normal, and his chest was free and light once more ... because the humidity had broken, yes, partially ... but more so because adrenaline had kicked in.

On this night he makes a beeline for Lake Huron, his eyes constantly drawn to the massive height of dark billowing cloud somersaulting over itself – a tidal wave of vapour breaking and crashing on the air. Most other vehicles are in retreat, heading in the sensible direction away from the storm. And those that aren't have at least pulled over to wait out the cloudburst's worst.

He pulls over momentarily to make some mental calculations. Given the distance and southwest trajectory of the system he estimates the front making direct landfall further down the shoreline, somewhere around Pyette Beach. He figures he will have fifteen minutes at the most to get there in time.

~

From her driver's seat, Erin peered out at the solitary figure pacing back and forth. Her white cover-up seemed almost to glow against the fading light of the storm as it billowed out and around

Meg's torso like a makeshift tent. At first Erin thought she would not bother reading it straight away. Given the increasing rain and wind, she had fully expected to see the woman give up and tuck the pages under her garments and head for the shelter of home. *Wherever that is.* And perhaps Meg would have indeed chosen that option after a paragraph or two had not something caught her eye – something that, in short order, quite literally stopped her in her tracks.

When her strides did continue, they were shorter, executed with rounded, tightened shoulders – the same shoulders Erin had observed the day they walked the length of the beach. But the curvature was now far more pronounced. She was hunched defensively, and not just because of the weather. The pages were gripped in both hands, pulled taut in front of the woman's eyes. Erin watched as Meg scrutinized one particular section for what seemed a dreadfully uncomfortable length of time. Then watched as she frantically shuffled back to a previous page, before returning again to the problematic passage. Meg stopped again. Wiped rainfall from her eyes. If it was rainfall. Then there was more intermittent pacing as she read on. Such was the pattern for the next ten minutes or more, a pattern that, as the moments ticked by, Erin could only bring herself to take in partially, with quick side glances from her now slumped position in the car. *Why in God's name did you force her hand like this? What the hell were you thinking?*

She had miscalculated. She knew it by the way her stomach had started to churn. She started up the car, but couldn't bear to leave. So she closed her eyes. Folded herself further down into the car seat, drew her knees to her chest and buried her head. By the time the pounding on the side window began, she was actually facing the other way, her entire body curled up below the view of anyone else passing by. Above the roaring wind, Meg's voice cut as jagged as if she had shattered the glass with her fist. "What the fuck is this! What the actual fuck is this?" From her periphery Erin could make out the ink-drenched pages, scrunched up like a firecracker in Meg's other hand, shaking and fluttering in the churning air. Then, with one last slam – one full body-check against the door itself, accompanied by the echo of a closing *FUCK YOU!* – she was gone.

~

Pyette Beach Up-To-Date Admin

It's really starting to blow out there. Reports of trees down further up the shoreline and power is out on the Bruce Peninsula. Tornado watch in effect according to Environment Canada and the Weather Channel. Be careful out there folks.

Randall Harwood

Still a few kite surfers out there as of five o'clock. They live for days like this.

Mitch Young

until the funnel clouds show up :(

Beth Armstrong

Stay safe everybody!

Deck furniture skidded across patios, shingle signs for restaurants and boutiques alike windmilled, while stray umbrellas, dislodged from their moorings, corkscrewed into the air. Trees bent, flags ripped and Erin Leith sped down Lakefront Drive looking for the first available turn to take her away from the storm. Then suddenly, for the second time that day, she cranked her steering wheel one hundred and eighty degrees, and headed back in the opposite direction. Once again, the decision was completely impulsive, though this second instance was borne entirely from the need to make amends for the consequences of the first. But with no phone number or address, no last name for this supposed friend, she found herself returning to the only place that presented itself as an option. With her car sending plumes of spray past the height of her hood, she hydroplaned her way back out to the beach, back to the spot she had just vacated moments before, this time parking to face the lake's onslaught head-on.

She had done damage. She had acted dangerously. The venom of Meg's face, imprinted in her mind, had made that perfectly clear. But the full panic of this realization would not arrive for a few more seconds – not until she looked up and through the cascading wall of water on her windshield to make out the vague outline of a figure in what looked like a white cotton cover-up, striding and stumbling erratically towards the breakwater.

~

His pulse has quickened again. By the time he pulls into the deserted parking lot he can feel it reverberating in his neck and his arms. He pulls the van as close to the sand as he can, facing the lake. He's just in time to see the roll shelf descend on top of him like a tumbling mountain range. It's only seven o'clock, but the mass of cloud has darkened the sky to nightfall. With the first microburst, sheets of rain actually shake his vehicle as much, if not more than the wind's velocity. And then, from that suffocating charcoal cloak, the sky strangely lightens to a faded green. He knows what will follow. He scans the water from north to south, out as far as what little daylight there is will allow. Looks for the tell-tale dark spots on the angry surface that so often this kind of strange and ominous sky foreshadows. Looks for spiral patterns, any possible spray twisting into a ringed pattern ... a funnel.

He fumbles with his headset – flips it on and calls up a refresh of the imaging on the laptop. The screen lights up with a map of Lake Huron overlaid with wild patterns depicted in fiery reds and sun-blazed yellows – ironic hues given the bleak slate-grey mayhem they represent. He speed-dials the CanWarn centre in preparation for a running commentary on this storm of a lifetime he has the fortune to witness first-hand. Then his eyes are back out over the water. He reports on two water spouts that appear slightly to the south of his location. Confirms they have touched down on the water, and appear to be heading parallel to the shore. He even attempts some rudimentary trigonometry to estimate their heights.

Because of this, he pays very little attention to the shore itself and does not immediately notice the five or six brave souls with pullovers and rain slicks soaked and pasted to their bodies. Does not take note of their frantic actions as they scream fruitlessly into the teeth of the storm, gesticulating wildly in the direction of the breakwater. No, not until tentacles of lightning begin their rapid-fire assault on the sky, their broken-glass patterns flashing relentlessly against a negative canvas, will the strobe image of a woman out on the dock clinging to a mooring post, register in his sight.

Chapter Five

~1~

"If we're all here and settled, I think we'll get started," Doreen announced. "I hope you all had a chance to read through Erin's submission. And, Erin, thanks for stepping into the fire with both feet. Wow."

Erin nodded weakly, keeping her eyes fixed on the end of her pen, which she flicked nervously. She had made the decision to continue with the writers' group exactly one week after the storm, the same day she had emailed her letter of resignation to her principal, the school board's human resources department and her union rep. The latter had been the most understanding, though beholden to his office in suggesting she might be better served to ask for a leave of absence and keep her options open, and her pension flowing. But on this her mind was already thoroughly made up – far more than it had been about submitting her composition to the group. Her hand had hovered over the send key on her laptop intermittently for the better part of the previous afternoon, retracting several times to make tea, feed the cat, pull some weeds from a front garden that she had not tended to all summer long. Until finally, with held breath and the tap of a finger, all of her late-night excerpts went soaring virtually in one file under the title *Between the Sand and the Sea*, with a subheading, *Variations on a Character Sketch*, which she had added hastily as an afterthought. She had hoped it would make the piece sound more literary, but now, after it flew through the ether, it felt more like she had hedged her bets with some sort of disclaimer.

She had been first to arrive, deliberately coming ten minutes early so she could stake out a defined territory ahead of the others. She selected the chair furthest from the door. Once seated, she set out her journal, her pens, and her phone in an arc around her – a buffer of sorts, or at least objects at her disposal to distract her from whatever criticisms might be fired her way.

"So ... to get the ball rolling, I'd just like to say I found this a fascinating read, Erin. I mean, having these juxtaposed character sketches laid out one after the other, sometimes expanding, sometimes turning right around and giving a completely different take. You've managed to create these little literary portraits of a complex woman, from very different vantage points in very different settings. Work, rest and play ... *definitely* play. Very inventive."

To her right, Avril Lawrence had already folded her hands and blown out her cheeks in a long low breath. The early timing of her entry into the fray was cause for concern to Erin. It had her thinking the woman wanted to get the piece out of the way, in favour of some topic of more interest. "I think ..." Avril began slowly, then after one more performative pause ... "I think I was most intrigued by the restaurant section. Your character ... um ..."

"Megan."

"Yes, thank you." She closed her eyes to demonstrate focus. "I *appreciated* reading about a character who in her role as a waitress – a role that society by and large would consider mundane – lowly, if you will – is able to take in fully her surroundings like a sponge. I *enjoyed* her ability to step back and understand the polar opposite reactions to the same setting of her beach community. From the rose-coloured paradise descriptions of the backpackers, to the jaded locals."

"Well, really it's more or less a take on Lewis's *Main Street*, right? Two characters passing with diametrically opposed vantage points of a common location." The speaker was Barry. "So I'm with the others to a point here, Erin. But, I have to say ... I'm not sure there's a real integration between the various sketches." Erin had expected Barry to be first out of the gates and was working on a response in her head when Doreen interjected on her behalf.

"But doesn't the subtitle, *Variations on a Character Sketch,* denote that the intent is to present a decidedly un-integrated portrayal of this woman?"

"Yes, but to what purpose? That's what kept stirring around in my head as I muddled through."

"Muddled? Really, Barry?"

"Oh I mean no offence. The muddling could very well be the result of my own shortcomings," he said in a tone that had absolutely no one around the table believing he meant it. "Or maybe ..." he paused and shrugged with a wince. Leaning forward on his elbows he brought his palms together to rub.

"It's okay, go on," Erin said.

"Maybe it's an idea that's not fully fleshed out yet. The effect of non-integration is intriguing ... really it is. Exploring a kind of Everyman theme from a feminist and post-feminist perspective ... *Everywoman,* I guess we should say. She's a waitress. She's a reluctant activist. She cuts loose big time in the city. But wait, all of a sudden you throw in she has a kid back home with grandma ..." He shuffled through the pages in front of him.

"Kyle."

"Right, Kyle." He leaned back in his chair and folded his arms. "But I guess what I'm missing here, is the *why. Why* have you have developed these rival perceptions of this character?"

"Because that's how people really are, Barry," the Presbyterian woman cut in. "Why can't one woman just be all these completely separate things at different times? Why *wouldn't* she?"

Yvonne nodded and stabbed the air with her pen in approval. "Or at the very least, she would be perceived diametrically by different people with their own varying sensibilities," she added.

Erin could not keep from letting a slight grin leak from her face. She glanced to the side to see that Doreen was sporting one as well.

"Reminds me of that old expression," piped up a tall man with a sweater knotted over his shoulders. He only showed up for sessions sporadically. No one was quite sure why. He brought no notes or papers or resources with him. But when in attendance, he could be counted on to sit with his arms folded and deliver at least one inopportune comment per session. "How does it go?" he continued. "'A woman should be a maid in the living room, a cook in the kitchen and a whore in the bedroom.' Who said that?" He leaned towards the Presbyterian woman. "Mick Jagger's wife, wasn't it?"

Yvonne rolled her eyes and carried on. "I also thought the way you illuminated the character's suspicions of being used for tokenism in the protest section was quite insightful."

"I will second that whole-heartedly," Doreen added, which prompted a sigh and abrupt shifting of weight from the seat next to Erin.

"Natasha?" Doreen asked from over the top of her reading glasses. The teenager squirmed a few seconds further, picking up her pencil to doodle on the inside cover of her notebook before responding.

"Well ... I mean ... 'said the white woman to the other white woman,' right?"

There was an awkward silence as the rest of the room exchanged glances until Doreen took it upon herself to seek clarification.

"You didn't find it a plausible depiction?"

"It's not for me to say," she replied, working her pencil a little harder.

Yvonne spoke up next. "So are you saying you don't believe it's okay for Erin to include a character from an ethnicity or race different from her own?"

"If her own race has been the dominant one for generations and generations, no ... I don't. Sorry."

"Even if it's written respectfully?"

Natasha stopped her sketching and let her hands slap against the table. "Even that question reeks of a completely colonialist mentality. All stories like this do is pile on top of centuries of writing where oppressed people are spoken for, and depicted by the literature and the voice of their oppressor."

Doreen folded her hands and rested her chin on them. "All right, then can I ask this?" she said slowly. "Do you believe that in this specific instance ..." she tapped her copy of Erin's story, "... even by drawing out a character who is concerned about being the object of tokenism, Erin, as the author, is herself guilty of tokenism?"

"If someone reads that character's opinions as the prevailing ethos of her particular culture, then yes ... because it reads like an excuse to deny that culture their empowerment."

"Oh I don't think anyone took it that way," Yvonne jumped in again quickly, her tone dripping with an insinuated *dear* which even Erin herself couldn't deny.

Natasha shrugged off the comment undaunted. "I'm sorry, but again ... 'said the white woman to a room full of white folks.'" Her pencil was back in her hand, going faster than ever. Erin glanced over and down to make out her sketch. It was a starburst explosion, with shards and lines and stars exploding off in all directions from the centre of the page, where a trio of words had been had been drawn in three-dimensional block letters, stacked one on top of the other.

APPROPRIATE
INAPPROPRIATE
IN-APPROPRIATION

"I guess you have to be the gay black unborn endangered whale, to write about the gay black unborn endangered whale," said the sweater-man who then shrugged in response to the silent, curious stares. He leaned in towards the Presbyterian woman once more. "That's a quote too ... can't remember who, though. Definitely not Mrs. Jagger this time," he chuckled. "Probably not Mick either, come to think of it. He'd have been too busy singing about his *Brown Sugar* and the like."

~2~

Seven days prior, and six blocks inland from the storm-ravaged shore, Megan Solomon pawed through the junk drawer in the kitchen of her apartment, stopping every few seconds to squeeze her fists and shake out her fingers. Sudden changes to the weather always affected her limbs and joints, so a wild squall like the one pounding against the windowpanes made the pain and stiffness inevitable. Some of it was arthritis, some from the pins and the rod.

Eventually her hand found what she had been groping for – the smooth tapered cylinders of her own hand-dipped candles. She pulled out one, then located a second rolling towards the back of the drawer. She scratched down the wax of both to expose the wick, all the while continuing to curse herself over the ridiculousness of not having more immediately at hand. (What was that saying about the shoemaker's children going barefoot?) She patted at the pockets of her jeans, looking for her lighter, then remembered seeing a matchbox left on the windowsill over the sink. She fumbled for it in the dark. Struck a flame and lit the wicks, then moulded both candles to a pair of saucers she had felt for in the drainboard, melting down the bottoms to adhere to the porcelain. She placed one on the kitchen table. For the second, she vacillated between bedroom and bathroom and it was during that back and forth of indecision that her flame illuminated the stack of waterlogged pages, sitting on the hall table.

It was such a blur – a completely unsettling turn of events from which she was still in shock. She deposited the makeshift candleholder on the bathroom vanity and returned to her table by the window, grabbing the papers on her way by.

Though she had no desire to revisit them, she found herself spreading them out in a haphazard collage, palms pressing each sheet out flat against the table top. She sat back to let the flickering light play over them, faintly satisfied by their disarray. Her eyes fell to the page closest to her, the excerpt at the dance club. *With my legs open for business, thank you very much.* For a moment she considered holding the sheet to the flame, but instead became entranced by the translucence of the paper's stock, and the way the candle backlit the type in a golden orange. This was followed by an acute awareness of the drip pattern forming down the side of her taper – both observations thanks, no doubt, to the full edible she had popped on her way home from the beach ... to deal with the oncoming aches and pain. And to get her past this brand new episode of shit.

'*But why are you so angry?*' she heard herself say just as the first spasms descended down her shin, causing her to cry out and slap the table. On cue, her three-year-old beagle came running from under her bed, marginally emboldened by the light the candle provided to risk jumping up into his owner's lap, and comforting her with the time-tested act of burrowing a nose into the folds of her hoodie. One of Meg's hands found the fine velvet fur just ahead of the animal's floppy ears – her favourite part. Slowly she rolled it between her thumb and forefinger. With the other hand, she checked her phone again, looking for any updates regarding the restoration of power. If the outage were to last into the morning she should get to the shop early. Set up some displays on tables outside – some tea light packages or maybe some of the beeswax – for those worried about a second night without electricity, if the power was indeed still out. Or if restored, for the vigilantly prepared looking to restock their supply for the next storm.

Another wave of pain hit her, this one descending from her hip. She dropped the phone to steady the dog. It landed beside Erin's writing, screen up. She found herself staring at both together – Megan Solomon imagined and in real life. Her phone shone with a sunset selfie taken early that summer out on the beach she so loved. The beach that had been her refuge and sanctuary, ever since the accident. Ever since crossing paths with one poorly placed buck on the highway between Little Current and Espanola, coming home from her cousin's wedding on Manitoulin. Since then, running had been out. Softball too. So swimming had been the alternative. Another reason to love the beach. She slid out a couple more pages from the bottom of the pile, read some of the passages about *her* being at odds with her native heritage. Being hesitant to participate in a protest to protect the beach.

"*What the fuck does she know about me?*" she snapped at the shadows. *This* was why she was so angry. Because Erin had used her. Because she had had the audacity to create some fantasy version of someone else's life for her own amusement and, worse yet, had the *complete* audacity to present it like some sort of gift.

Meg squeezed the throbbing from her fingers and wrists once more and vowed she would not apologize for the way she was, or the way she lived. And she would not bend to this passive-aggressive manipulation ... this obvious attempt to coax her skeletons into the light of day, divulging every nook and cranny of her past, every fear and anxiety along the way. Because look where that had got her. Used and chewed up and spit out. Abandoned by the very people whom she thought would care. People who should have cared. Who should've had her back. And yes, she had survived, but the price of survival was high. She would never be the open book that Erin seemingly craved she was. She would never default to trust. Everything was a calculation. Everything needed to be tactical and measured. Transactional only. She would not get hurt again. She would not put herself in that position. And no, obviously everyone wasn't capable of the abuse she had experienced. Certainly not Erin. But at the same time, everyone wasn't up to the task of understanding what surviving had entailed. The daily routine of hiding bruises. Long sleeves on hot summer days. Tensor bandages over cuts and abrasions. *Just a sprain. I jammed it playing ball.* Sunglasses on the cloudiest of mornings to hide the blackened eyes. *I have a migraine, it helps.* Jumping from a moving vehicle to finally get away. *That moose came out of nowhere.*

Of course, Erin posed no threat or danger. Nothing like it. But the past – the muscle memory of the torment would always be just one tap on the shoulder away. And as Meg panned over the sheets of her own personal fiction, she could not help feeling vulnerable. Triggered even. Because it was clear Erin's goal with this writing had been to prod the real Megan out in the open. Had she only realized she already *had* the real Megan right there in front of her eyes the whole time – a woman who, yes, may be spontaneously tactile, but who would always remain reserved about the details of her past.

And just what right did she have to transparency anyway? A woman with a wedding ring who sneaks off for a lesbian romp on the beach every weekday afternoon. Was that supposed to inspire Meg to bare her soul? Shouldn't it have done the exact opposite? Shouldn't the red flags have been out and flying in the gale-force winds? How could Erin think they were anything more than an extra-curricular hook-up? Was she actually considering uprooting her marriage and her life for somebody she liked the look of in a swimsuit ... as if there was a connection anything more than physical? More than something born of restlessness, or boredom, *or who knows the fuck what?* But then to have all of this insecurity cloaked in her literary bullshit where *I'm* the one with my legs open for strangers. *I'm* the one at odds with my heritage. At odds with my upbringing and my history ...

With Meg's anger rising again, Erin's pages found their way to the floor. Launched by a swipe of the arm, they fluttered momentarily above the candle's glow before floating down into the shadows below the flame. The startled dog jumped from her lap and, with the scratching of paws across paper and then tile, scampered back down the hallway. Then, for the first time, not just since the blow-up with Erin on the beach, but the first time in as long as she could remember, Meg felt a tear escape from the outside corner of her left eye. Then another. It was an unfamiliar feeling and it irritated her. But like scratching a rash, her mad attempts to clear it away only seemed to serve to supply the flow with reinforcements – out of both eyes now, flooding her vision. She dropped her head to the table and surrendered to the onslaught, suddenly aware that her shoulders had started to heave. At first she strained to control the movement – lock the muscles from her elbows back to her neck. But it was to no avail, as this too only seemed to exacerbate the involuntary spasms. She sprang to her feet and screamed into the dark as she pounded her fists on the table, causing the dog to claw his way further under a bed. "No! Don't fucking do this!" she seethed, grabbing a red and blue windbreaker. Yanking on a pair of hiking boots that sat ready at the door despite having not seen any action since mid-May, she pulled a baseball cap down over her brow and bolted out the apartment door, down the stairs, and out into the raging night.

~3~

"I did like your title, though." Natasha peeked up from underneath her shock of purple-black hair. "*Between the Sand and the Sea*. Because it's an impossibility, right?"

"Yup," Erin replied and though the implication was completely of her own design, she felt a hint of despair hearing it repeated back to her out loud. Then came Barry again.

"I suppose you could liken it to Maugham's *The Razor's Edge,* as far as titles go. However, I have to say – if we're being specific – from the scene with the sand dunes and the restaurant, it's clear you've set this out at Pyette Beach, which would be a lake, and not a sea. Perhaps that's splitting hairs ..."

"Yes, perhaps," Doreen said, letting her response linger slowly off her lips without looking up.

Other points were raised. Yvonne noted how Erin had saved the introduction of her character's name until partway through the whole piece. The Presbyterian lady had quite liked that particular effect, and had also appreciated how each section of the composition had increased in size and detail. "Like building a pyramid from the top down," she said. "Or you could think of the opening sections as just the tip of an iceberg and you've dared to dive below into the cold and the dark to see what's underneath. I mean, these first sections are just a few tantalizing sentences but they're mysterious, aren't they? And they build and build to make this multi-layered intriguing personality right up to your final scene, with all her struggles ... her downfall, I guess you could say ..."

Erin listened as Natasha jumped in to defend Meg's reputation. Yvonne did likewise, wondering whether the last section was even intended to be the final definitive word on the character. Discussion rattled around the room for another fifteen minutes or so until, due to the constraints of format, the group moved on to the requisite writing prompts and exercises, followed by a brief discussion of one of Natasha's poems she had written freehand beneath the sketch of a young girl in workboots and sunglasses leaning against a fence. Photocopies had been distributed for the group to consider.

An hour later Erin was reaching for her handbag, to return her pen and journal, with a tangible but unforeseen sense of ambivalence. An emptiness from having emptied herself, perhaps. One by one the writers packed up their belongings and headed out the door, Barry and the church lady first – still at odds and hammering out more details of Erin's story. Then Natasha, followed quickly by Doreen, who wanted a word with the teen before she disappeared. Soon Erin was alone again in the room, save for Doreen's mother, tucked into an armchair in the far corner. She often tagged along, but rarely spoke and never participated during class. "I write a little bit of verse," she had confided on Erin's first-ever session. "About my flower gardens or the changing seasons, but certainly nothing like you lot discuss. Still ... it's an outing, I guess.

Erin wasn't even aware she was still in the room, having spun her chair to stare up through the lone window towards the one visible tree branch tapping lightly against the pane. So she jumped in her seat when the woman's sudden sneeze reverberated between the room's walls.

"Oh, Mrs. Lemke, I didn't see you–"

The woman waved her off. "My fault, my fault," she said, leaning forward at full stretch to reach for a box of Kleenex on the table, before collapsing with a thud back onto her chair. "Just waiting on Doreen, per usual. May as well stay here 'til she comes back for her things." She gestured towards her daughter's purse and notebook. Erin nodded and smiled, then spun back towards the window.

"You don't seem in any hurry either," the woman noted.

"I guess not." Erin had hoped to catch Doreen for a few minutes more – possibly delve a little deeper into her mentor's thoughts on her piece. But with her mother present, it now appeared likely that waiting for that opportunity would involve an awkward silence in the interim. And while silence, in and of itself, was a comfortable state for Erin as a rule, silence with an audience was another matter. She had just nicely pulled herself up out her chair to leave when the elderly woman spoke again, daring to ask the simple question that not one of Erin's peers had managed or even entertained the notion of posing.

"Can you tell me about your story, dear?" she said. It had come out so simply and disarmingly that, ten minutes later, Erin was curled up in the chair next to the woman, divulging the entire inspiration for the character in her sketches. She described how they had met on the beach. How, despite Erin being married, she had entertained Meg's advances, and reciprocated in kind. She even confessed to being unable to stop thinking about Meg, and being unable to return to going through the motions of the life she had previously managed for years and years. She explained how each character sketch was written at night when she couldn't sleep, when either guilt or excitement, or some combination of the two had kept her up, and the only semblance of solace she could eke out were these little vignettes that merely *imagined* what the rest of Meg's life must have been like. "So ... in the absence of getting to know her as well as I wanted ... I guess you could say I extrapolated."

"Well ..." Doreen's mother said, nodding and staring at her hands folded in her lap. "That is very interesting. But I should confess. I did read your story. Doreen lets me, now and again. I hope that's okay."

"Fine by me," Erin replied with a shrug, but then on further consideration, spun around to face the elderly woman. "So what did *you* think of it then?"

"Well, ... at the time I wondered whether all of these different versions of Meg you described weren't actually just different sides of you."

Erin pulled her legs up in the chair, and grabbed onto her toes. "Well, no ... I mean, I don't have any native heritage, and my daughter is grown up and off to college," she said, before quickly adding, "but I'd be interested to know why would you have thought that."

The woman shrugged. "I don't know ... just a feeling. Something about the way each section seemed maybe a little bit angrier than the last?"

Chapter Six

Local Woman Dies In Wednesday's Storm

The body of a local woman was found washed ashore on Pyette Beach early Thursday morning. Naomi 'Minnie' Coture of no fixed address was discovered by passers-by shortly before 10:00 a.m. Ms. Coture is believed to have been residing in a cabin at The Breakers Campground for the past few weeks.

Coture was known to spend her days along the shore and many had witnessed her walking the beach, as well as past the moorings in the yacht club and out on the town's breakwater. She was known for her trademark white pant suits and bright smile. Neighbours at The Breakers described her as a friendly happy-go-lucky woman who loved to be out in public.

Police officials believe Ms. Coture likely ignored the warnings of threatening weather to complete her daily walk, and was swept into the water late Wednesday afternoon. Anyone who may have witnessed her whereabouts on that day is asked to contact the Pyette Beach OPP detachment.

~1~

Erin stood facing the chain-link fence. It was eight feet high with several 'Danger – Keep Out' placards tied along its length at regular intervals. Beyond it, inaccessible, lay her swimming rock. She watched as the autumn waves crashed over its flat surface and pooled around the base where they had trapped a handful of soggy golden leaves. What were they? Beech? Birch? After forty-four years on the planet, she still didn't know. *Not maple* ... and *dead.* That was the best she could do. A writer – a *real* writer – would know one from the other. A *real* writer would differentiate with rich descriptions of their texture, shape and hue. All the authors she had ever admired were always up to the task of making such distinctions in fine literary fashion. Furthermore, a *real* writer would be able to extrapolate great meaning from the sight of a limp and lifeless leaf at the mercy of nature's demolition. They would find the beauty in such destruction. She wiped the blowing surf and grit from her eyes. It was only mid-September but already it felt like late autumn. Like a cold November morning.

November was the angriest month as far as Great Lakes history was concerned. She had learned this on the very first day of what now passed for employment – a temporary, part-time contract as the curator's assistant in the Pyette Beach Marine Museum. Minimum wage, but only a five-minute walk from where she now stood, which, if she was being honest with herself, had been the deciding factor for agreeing to the position. Because in truth, she could not summon even an ounce of sincere interest for the history and heritage that was so painstakingly preserved in the gallery's modest six rooms. And her indifference definitely clouded her perception. She found the place faintly dank, and there was a dimness to the lighting that seemed to dull rather than illuminate the display cases, all filled with yellowed pages and rusted artifacts, most of which she felt suffered from overcrowding. Each item vying with another for preciously scant space and attention. The past competing with the past. The dead-and-gone fighting the dead-and-gone. After a week, she had begun to feel a bit claustrophobic. Her chest was heavy and her breathing laboured (like Ross used to get when it was humid, she reminded herself). After two weeks, she actually started to loathe the job, and, at least once a day, had to fight the urge to run out the door screaming. Which should have come as no surprise. Even on the first day of her orientation, she had found the curator's voice possessed a droning quality that put his instruction far below her level of concentration, leaving her thoughts to meander aimlessly until they landed, curiously, on some vague notion she retrieved from her memory of a university elective over two decades before. *Religion as Literature*. From foggy recollection, she had conjured up a lecture about the minor prophets of the Old Testament, in which she had learned that those particular biblical writings, that dealt with events from the eighth to the fifth century BC, had actually not been written down and compiled until somewhere around 150 years before Christ. She remembered how this news had elicited a strangely restless feeling in her, because it suggested that perhaps no particular era would ever get an honest chance to record its own stories. That it would always be too busy operating as a scribe – a *museum* if you will – for what had come and gone centuries before. Too busy with its myths to sculpt out the here and now. That was as far as she got revisiting the notion, however, the reminiscing having come to an abrupt halt when the curator asked if she had any questions on the system for cataloguing collections that he had just gone over. By shaking her head, she was then the recipient of another monotone overview, this one concerning the institution's revamped procedure for procuring travelling exhibits.

Yes, November ... half of Lake Huron's shipwrecks occurred in November – from schooners to skiffs to side-wheelers, steamers and freighters. One storm alone in 1913 took down nineteen vessels. Over 250 lives plucked and chewed and swallowed by the lake's rage. It was a necessary evil of the shipping industry, the museum displays seemed to imply. Or at least that was the inference Erin drew the day she first scanned the miniature replicas of the fallen vessels, each looking as delicate in its glass case as the actual ships had proved to be against the thirty-five foot swells that had ripped them apart. Tragedies such as these were the price to pay for settling and subduing the rough and wild shoreline of a Great Lake. How else could her forefathers have ripped the timber from the landscape, or dragged the fish from their shoals to salt and send en masse throughout the continent? It was simply the understood price to pay for taming the wilderness into the genteel landscape for which it was now known. Rolling farmland. Quaint towns, that were once mere crossroads ... a sawmill here, a tavern there. And what about her beloved spacious beach front, built on the backs, the sweat, and the casualties of the rugged pioneering generations who had clear-cut it, hunted it out, overfished it, sold it ...?

Many of the exhibits' captions and plaques were not shy about chronicling how many of the first European settlers to the area had been Scottish – using an abundance of stereotypical descriptions of a people who singularly possessed the requisite rigour and tenacity to tame the bush lands of Upper Canada's frontier ... survivors as they were of a culled tenant farming class, shunned from their own limited homelands by landlords who favoured the grazing of sheep.

For the shipping barons and their captains of this hardy lineage (and indeed for the sailors and deck-hands, who toiled beneath them), was this the motivation for squeezing in one more boatload of commerce to Superior before winter ... one more run through Bruce Mines, Thessalon and The Soo before the winter freeze? To honour their thrifty and austere heritage? Or did their reasoning have more to do with straight-forward colonial capitalism ... their resolve owing far more to the margins in their ledgers than any gathering cloud formations out over the horizon. The rationale that if they didn't try one more run, someone else surely would. It would be money taken from their pockets. Business waved elsewhere that could have been theirs.

Or was it a bit of both? An industrious form of desperation ... but desperation nonetheless.

~

She cast her gaze further out into the lake to follow a particularly formidable wave as it rolled in towards shore. It barrelled over the government dock, sending tendrils of water under the fencing and up around the soles of her shoes. She linked her fingers through the fence. Gripped and squeezed, then shook the barrier as she stared out at her isolated rock, the spray once again lashing at her face and stinging her cheeks. From a distance she heard Avery's frantic footsteps running toward her – her voice intermittently audible between the pounding rhythm of the breakers. She had been home for two consecutive weekends now – an unprecedented occurrence. Home at the request of her father to devote some time to helping him *deal with her mother*.

"Jesus, Mom ... not again."

~2~

"So ... let's hear it. 'Cause you sure as hell didn't buy that for me."

Ross had laid out her swimsuit on their bedspread, smoothed out and arranged as if a chalk outline of her body had meant to be traced around it. She knew she had been lackadaisical, leaving it about the house for the past three weeks. In the laundry basket, or kicked under their clothes dresser. Part of her – despite the impossibility of it all – needed to do something to integrate the mutually exclusive worlds into which she had divided herself. Part of her needed to be found out – needed to come clean. Why, then, did she suddenly feel so profoundly unprepared for the reality of the moment, as she stood there beside him, her eyes not daring to look up from the bed? Her mouth was open but in no way ready to speak. She could no longer feel the tile floor beneath her feet. All sensation had been sucked inside – into a cold spasm that gripped her spine from neck to tailbone.

He claimed he had merely come upon the suit while searching for one of his folk club T-shirts – the monogrammed black one that had been given to him by the board of directors for ten years of service as their sound man. (God, how he cherished that shirt.) But surely there was more to it. Surely he was still fumbling to make sense of the night of the storm. Finding his wife deliriously clinging to a dock in the middle of the storm of the century should have already occasioned so much more of a response. And yet, on the evening in question, he had only concerned himself with her physical state. He had tended to her so professionally, as if she were a *perfect* stranger, gathering her into the blanket he kept in the van with the rest of his storm-chasing gear. That included a first aid kit from which he produced bandages to take care of cuts along her index finger and over her elbow, as well as iodine which he swabbed on a scrape down her left leg. There had been no questions about why she was out there in the first place. No interrogation as to why she had willingly put herself in harm's way. Why she had been so upset. Nothing was exchanged about how she had initially resisted his rescue efforts, and fought to remain clinging to the mooring peg, nor the way she had clawed at him, pounding his chest as he dragged her to safety. Even once they were home – when the *whys*, if not the *what the fucks* should have commenced in earnest – after a hot shower, and a change into flannels and a robe – when she had descended the stairs braced for the need to offer some sort of explanation, she found him under his headphones, back in his studio, his eyes locked on the wavelength patterns stretched across his computer screen – jagged undulations of red and blue and green. Lost in his own private musical storm.

The tenuous stasis remained for a week – a silent elephant living in their home, which ironically amounted to next to no change in the separate parallel lines that was their life.

Until now.

"Come on, Erin," he said, waving his hand over the bedspread. "Convince me everything's just absolutely A-fucking-OK."

She shrugged. "It's a swimsuit."

"Yeah I know. And when exactly have you been putting yourself in that little number?"

"I ordered it last May, with a bunch of stuff for Avery," she lied.

"But not for me–"

Her hands found her hips. "No, Ross. For me. *Me*." She was aware how easily her voice had risen – *pre-intensified* – as if in a rush to catch up to an already-escalated argument that had been smouldering silently for such a long time that its unleashing felt like tinders reigniting. He felt it too. She could tell by his once-a-year tone, a rarely produced timbre absent in all but their most extreme arguments. What brief appearances it made had traditionally revolved around arguments over parenting.

Their daughter had always been headstrong, and she had long known how to take advantage of her father's aversion to confrontation. From early on, Avery had learned to use that antipathy to get her way in all matters of curfew, parties, dating, and general independence. All that was required was an unwavering air of righteousness accompanied by crossed arms and a determined stare that communicated how disappointed *she* was in *his* lack of trust of her own maturity and powers of good judgement. It had always worked to great effect. Ross would acquiesce, leaving the required tougher-love parenting from mum completely unreinforced. And by that point it was usually too late. Their good-cop, no-cop routine was simply not an effective response for dealing with the strength of will their daughter possessed. Ross's voice and ire only put in an appearance when and if Erin goaded it from his natural tacit state with a '*could you at least give me some hint as to what you're thinking.*'

She wondered if that's what he thought the swimsuit was all about – her low-cut, high-on-the-hip two-piece swimsuit. Perhaps he interpreted it as her daring him to stay silent. Daring him to remain unaffected. Daring him *not* to react and confront her with some latent old-testament wrath he didn't even realize he had been storing up.

"So what ... you wear this thing when I'm not around?"

"I wear it at the beach, obviously."

"And when exactly is that?"

They stared at each other for several moments until she strode forward, snatched up the suit from the bed and headed for the en suite hamper. "For Christ's sake, Ross, when was the last time you wanted a day at the beach?" It was a point that needed circumventing on his part, for in a marriage of limited shared pastimes the beach had been discarded long ago, dying out once their young daughter's urges for ice cream cones, and float toys had given way to the pleas of a teenager to let her hang out at her friend's house with the pool, and get a ride on her own ... ('Yes Dad, there will be boys' ... *sigh*. 'Yes, there'll be a bunch of us, but Britt will drive and you know her' ... *sigh*.)

"So who is he, Erin?"

"Who is who?" she said, conjuring up her best indignation, as she headed out the bedroom and down the hall for the kitchen.

"THE GUY!" he yelled, grabbing over her shoulder and spinning her around and up against the closet door. For an instant both were pinned there in shock, she by his unexpected force, he by the disbelief that he was capable of what he had just done. They stared wide-eyed at one another, her hands shaking because she could see the fists that had grabbed her wrists were doing likewise. It was the suddenness that frightened her the most. Ross had no practice dealing with anger. Neither of them did.

"Don't you ever fucking do that again–"

"Who the hell is he!"

"THERE IS NO GUY!"

"Really. So you just suddenly get the urge to parade around in public with your ass out."

She wrestled from his grip. Put her hands flat on his chest but didn't push him away. Instead she let her palms rest there as she momentarily stared at the backs of her hands, her fingers ... the wearisome never-ending circle that was her wedding ring. For a second she felt as small as she ever had in her marriage. But then another emotion took charge, in reaction to the first, overtaking the inertia of apathy on which her house and home ... and life … had too long been based. She raised her eyes to meet his and she could feel her lip begin to quiver.

"That's right, Ross. That's exactly the urge I get," she seethed, and shoved him back into the wall. Grabbing her purse, she kicked open the front door. The last words he heard from her that day were something to the effect that she would continue to do so whenever she fucking felt like it.

~3~

The wind had freshened that evening and rolled the cloud cover out into the lake, raising the curtain on a vibrant sunset that had been missing from the horizon since the end of August. The change in weather brought out a sampling of the beach's population, sparse by summer's standards – mostly buttoned-up walkers with dogs in tow, a few brave children still eager to wade and splash for all they were worth, oblivious to the fading day's rays – and one mother with her adult daughter, both ambling slowly with hands in pockets, both with periodic glances from their shoe tops out across the water. Neither spoke any words of substance until they had completed a full length of the beach, down and back, to find themselves again at the base of the now inaccessible breakwater.

"Dad says you're sleeping around," Avery finally began, plopping herself down cross-legged on the sand without the use of her hands still nestled deep in the pouch pocket of her hoodie. Erin stared down at her daughter, then without a reply, joined her. "So are you?"

From a very early age Avery Morton had refused to stand on ceremony. Almost instinctively she had eschewed every variety of small talk and pleasantry as wasted effort, so Erin accepted the question as it was intended – a straight-ahead, shortest-distance-needed approach to getting on with the issue at hand. It had dawned on Erin that of all the people affected by this whole messy chaotic equation, her daughter just might be the one who could handle it better than anyone else – Erin included. But it was an impression that the mother in her could not help fight. Surely her daughter's youth and her black-and-white view of the world would make her experiences a subset of her own. That was the natural order of things, after all, was it not? So what advantage could be gained from Avery lending an ear? Or an opinion? And yet this had always been her daughter's strength. Yes, her un-nuanced approach found its limitations from time to time, but it also proved her unsusceptible to the great amounts of bullshit that passed for most people's messy ambivalent way of meandering through life. Had she not always been favoured counsel for so many a friend on so many an occasion? Perhaps with simplicity came clarity. Couples fight. Couples grow apart. Couples sometimes cheat and struggle. Sometimes they lie to each other. Her parents were a couple. Therefore perhaps all of this mess was, in fact, a reasonable possibility in her daughter's mind.

"So ...?"

Erin nodded. "There's a woman," she said.

Avery studied her mother's profile with a look so lacking in shock or surprise it broke Erin's gaze on the lake. For a second she almost expected her daughter to nod back at her and tell her she had suspected as much. "By the way, how did you know I'd be here?" she asked.

"It's the third place I looked, actually. I checked Sauble and Southampton first. Dad said you'd probably head for the beach."

"Sent you to do his bidding, did he?"

Their eyes were locked for a moment until Erin had to glance away.

"So tell me about her, Mom."

Erin shook her head, kicked out her feet. "Oh, Aves ... I can't–"

"Why not?"

"Because it's cheating." She said this with her eyes wide and tearing. "I've been cheating on your father. And you. I've had this ... this affair right under your noses, and I mean, Meg – that's her name – she just became part of this other version of me so fast, and so ... easily. But while she's over here, there's you and your dad, and real life, and responsibilities and a house, and the world in general over there, so–"

She had to stop. It all sounded too preposterous, and raw, these words falling from her mouth. She had no choice but to let the explanation trail away, lost in the relentless rhythm of shore-bound breakers. So they just sat, mother and daughter. One inert with legs stretched out straight, heels dug into the sand. One drawn up into a ball, knees under chin, with hands fidgeting at the sleeve cuffs of her windbreaker, which she used to mop her face. After a good length of silence Avery Morton reached out a hand to smooth some hair away from Erin's face.

"So move me over."

"What?"

Avery got up and squatted in front of her mother, arms still folded to her chest, eyes still boring into Erin's thoughts. "Well ... you say you've split yourself in two. Clearly something has to give. So, for a start, why not move me over?"

Tears were coming freely now. Erin shook her head. "No. No way. I do *not* deserve that kind of consideration. There's absolutely no excuse for–"

"Mom!" She bent lower to peer up under her mother's fallen face. Lifted her chin the way Erin imagined she would one day to her own daughter. "Because here's the thing," she said. "I'll be fine whether you and dad get through this or not. Yeah, it would kind of suck if you couldn't, but I can deal with it. Besides, half of my friends' parents aren't together either. You know that."

Erin let out a long slow breath and closed her eyes. "So what exactly do you want to know?"

Avery lowered herself on the sand once more, spinning until she came to lean against her mother's shoulder. "I want you to tell me all about your girlfriend."

"Aves, come on ... look, I'm not even sure how much ..." The words trailed off again.

"... how much she's into you? Well, welcome to the friggin' world, Mom."

For the next hour, while the sun dipped past the waves and the deepest hues of the western sky faded through its oranges and reds towards a purple-grey, Erin confided in her daughter. She began with the original flight of fancy to the beach, her confession of the freedom she felt from being alone, of being nowhere and *no one* in particular. How, at first, it had just been for an afternoon –- a one-off – but had grown into something she tried again and again until the sand and water became her refuge. Refuge from what, her daughter wanted to know, which Erin took not as accusatory, but as the curiosity of someone who truly had yet to know the possibility of needing such a place – someone who probably would never have any interest in pursuing a life that might one day necessitate fleeing from her own choices. This was what Erin loved about her daughter the most. That she was everything her mother was not – everything Erin could not help being scared of.

"And another thing. Let's talk about your swimsuit of choice, Mother-dear. Would it be that black two-piece I saw in the wash?" And so for a little while at least they retreated to talk about beach wear – cuts and styles – with Erin asking her thoughts on what was in, what Avery liked. She confessed how good Meg looked in hers, and described her swimmer's physique. How she seemed so athletic and streamlined in the water.

"So have you ever liked girls before?" Avery then asked. Strangely, it was a question to which her mother had given precious little attention. Because the truth was, she had not. More comfortable around them, yes, she admitted, especially when she was younger. "But then again, I was pretty much a hermit at university. Friends were always trying to pry me from a book to go out for a night on the town, or a house party somewhere. I think I looked as nice as the next girl, but didn't really carry it, you know?" She tried to explain that, back then, she truly preferred a good novel to the pressures of socializing. "Still do, I guess."

"Any crushes on the women in your books then?"

Erin leaned back on her palms and stretched her legs out straight. She cocked her head, marvelling at her daughter's gift of insight. This too was her beautiful Avery, sitting steadfast and independently, probing her mother's psyche in one breath, discussing how much cheek she liked to show at the beach the next. Apologizing for none of it. So natural and comfortable in her own skin. *And none of it of your doing.*

She kept her eyes trained, watching her daughter glow in the dwindling daylight, confident that Avery's straightforward approach to seeing the world owed nothing to *naïveté* or inexperience. Rather, in her daughter, Erin suspected she was witnessing evolution exuded – a version of womanhood on its way to being truly better than herself.

"You're doing that staring thing, Mom."

Erin turned back to the darkened lake and sighed. "I guess we should talk about your dad and me a bit more," she said.

"Here's an idea. How about you two talk to each other?"

"Yeah? Should I tell him how good Meg looks in her bikini?"

Avery pivoted. "I mean it, Mom."

"So does that mean you won't be saying anything to him then?" Immediately she wished she hadn't blurted it out. It had sounded so feeble. So childish. They stared once more at one another until Avery shifted back towards the water, digging her heels into the damp sand. "I won't bring it up. But I won't hide it either," she replied.

"Can't count on kids these days."

"Damn it, Mom, knock it off! I'm serious. Britt got caught in the middle of her parents' divorce–"

"Divorce? Who said anything about–"

"Well, if you're keen to explore your inner lesbian, I'm guessing Dad's probably gonna make other plans."

Erin blew out her cheeks ... picked up a handful of sand and sifted it through her fist. "Truth is, I'm not even sure that's what has him so mad."

"Um ... yeah, Mom. Trust me. That's what has him so mad."

"Yes, alright, alright ... what I mean is ... for years we've been living like no more than room-mates. Co-managers of a home and finances ... looking after the place, getting you off to college. Work and all of his bloody hobbies. Christ we haven't had sex in–"

"Geez, Mom, do you have to?"

"You said, *move me*, kiddo. Welcome to the other side."

Avery got up, slid her hands into the back pockets of her cut-offs and turned to stand in front of her mother, her eyes distant, her mind at work. Erin reached for her sleeve to bring her back closer. "What are you thinking?" she wanted to know.

Avery shrugged, letting her arms fall to slap her sides. "I'm thinking you want to leave him."

"Avery!"

"Or you want him to decide to leave you."

"But, Aves, you love your dad."

"Of course I love my dad. I love you too. So what? It's not about me. I mean, don't get me wrong, it would suck on a bunch of levels. But like I said, I'll be fine. Either way, I *will* be fine. Shit, it's not like I'm still nine years old." She began to pace a bit, stretching her arms up over her head and flexing her fingers, as if shaking her thoughts out through the ends of her limbs. "You said you're not sure if this Meg is into you ... but it sure as hell sounds like you and dad aren't into each other either anymore. So why not try separate ways?"

With the rawness of the question, posed like some rudimentary puzzle-book solution, Erin reversed her opinion on the matter of her daughter – a complete about-face on the counsel before her. It was just too simplistic a take on the situation. Avery's youth had betrayed her. They were a family, and the years and effort invested in the life they had forged for themselves in their home and community, the comfort and stressless-ness of it – it was all too much for one restless summer to overcome. Clearly her daughter could not see that. Clearly her advice was aiming at a place she did not yet know, and hopefully never would. Because the thought of ending it all, in the cold fading light of an autumn evening did nothing but send a chill down her mother's back. It only served to prove the status quo was the easier pill to swallow. (*Side effects may include a growing numbness and the inability to feel any meaningful emotion.)* Forget the ship of new experiences and choices – that ship had sailed long ago. At issue was the path of least resistance for a tired but staid couple. This was about survival, not happiness.

"I mean, is it some sort of religious thing? Can't break the vows no matter what."

"Look, I really think you're getting ahead of yourself with this," Erin said quickly, even as the voice in her head observed she was dialling back the conversation for her own sake, not her daughter's. (*Or Ross's, for that matter.*)

The daughter shrugged and sat down again. "Or a stubbornness thing?" she continued. "The need to lord it over people like Britt's parents? Because, I mean, if that's all it is, then you guys are better off putting yourselves out of each other's misery. Instead of, like, you know ... suffering for your matrimony."

Each stared at her own feet a moment, peering down at the mounds of sand their toes and heels had constructed. "That's a good turn of phrase," Erin said eventually. "*Suffering for your matrimony*. You should try writing."

"Oh for Christ's sake, Mom!"

"Hey! Bear with me, kid. It's not like this is something I ever prepared for." Erin felt her posture slacken, her shoulders cave in on themselves, as though they were trying to follow her hands into her pockets.

"Okay, Okay. So in that case ... just take a breath, and tell me what you want to do next."

Erin stood up and focused once more on the rhythm of the waves rolling in one after the other, and somewhere in their cadence found her answer "What I want to do next?" she said. "Is scream, Aves. That's what I want to do next. I want to scream at the top of my fucking lungs!"

Avery glanced sidelong at her mother, and after lending her a moment's calm said, "But don't you think maybe all of this ..." She made a circular motion with her hand. "Don't you think it all might be you screaming?"

Erin blew the air from her cheeks again, and threw her head back, staring up into the growing night. "You know, there was a time ... when I was around your age ... *this* me would have been completely out of the question. I was the twenty-something who craved to be older and settled. Sought out the quiet small-town life. A simple home with tasteful vintage furniture. Thought that was what would see me through ... fulfil the image I had for myself. I got thinking about that the other day when I was reading. It was a novel about the life of this housewife from about your age right through to her eighties. In the last chapter she's widowed. So she moves from her small town into the city. Gets a high-rise apartment with lots of windows and views. Sells all her antiques and maple dinettes and furniture. Replaces it all with chrome tables and chairs and shelving. Paints the walls white and adds splashes of colour with modern abstract art pieces. 'Bright and shiny,' she says. Because that's what old age actually craves ... something bright and shiny. Something new."

Erin paused to pull the hood up on her windbreaker, resisting the urge to do the same for her daughter. "I have a confession," she said.

"Another one?"

"Just hear me out, okay?" She paused for several deep breaths. "I don't think I really know you." A squint was the only reply, so she continued. "I love you completely. And I am in absolute awe of your one-hundred-percent no bullshit, cut-to-the-heart-of-the-matter approach to life. But that's also the problem. Because the truth is, I can't measure up to it, Aves. I can't relate."

"Mom, come on–"

"No, you have to hear this. You see, while I marvel at your problem-solving, and your intelligence ..." She reached up and grabbed onto a handful of her daughter's jacket, giving it a bit of a shake. "I don't really know what's soft and comfortable in there. Name me a memory that you hold on to. Something you think you'll always treasure and think fondly of for years to come."

Avery shrugged. "I don't know ... like what?"

"Anything. Big or small ... your brain-teasers with your father maybe."

"God, Mom."

"What?"

"I'm twenty-one. Don't you think that's something I should be letting go of, not hanging on to?"

Erin nodded and looked away. "Maybe so," she said quietly.

"I mean, I love you too, but maybe this is just where we're a bit different."

"Maybe," her mother agreed. "Or maybe to feel nostalgic, you have to be returning to something ... something you've left behind and didn't realize you missed until it was gone." She zipped her jacket up to the neckline, rolled her shoulders again to collect some more warmth. "Who knows? Maybe it's not even a fair question.

Maybe my own sense of nostalgia started later than where you're at now."

"Great. So I've got all this to look forward to?"

"Oh, sweetie, I doubt it. My guess is that if a scream ever needs to come out of that beautiful heart of yours, nothing's going to get in its way."

For quite a while the two were silent, each thinking privately that the encroaching darkness should bid their departure, but both also hoping the other would not move too soon, for the air was not yet too chilly, and the gentle rhythm of the water was a peaceful sound. So instead they leaned against one another, head to shoulder, arm hooked in arm.

"So ... your friend Meg," Avery said after several minutes had passed. "Is she part of the scream ... or is she what comes after?"

How she loved her daughter's mind.

~4~

Pedal-Steel Man

Just back from a month out on the road. Can anybody tell me when the bright lights that run the show decided to fence off the breakwater?

Celia Andersson

A woman was blown off the night of the storm.

Pedal-Steel Man

So they close the whole thing because of somebody's lack of judgement.

Celia Andersson

Pedal-Steel Man I believe they lost their life. The rumour is at least one other had to be rescued as well. Probably became a liability issue for the town.

Mitch Young

Pedal-Steel Man Welcome to the New World Order. Catering to the lowest common denominator.

~

Avery organized the meeting to be away from the house, where for the intervening two weeks there had been a cold silence hanging from the ceiling, a pressure system showing no sign of moving in any direction. Anywhere near the beach she felt should be off limits as well, even though it was the only place her mother had been spending any time, apart from her hours at the museum. She had come home from school to witness two endless clock-ticking weekends stretch uncomfortable minutes into hours, with each parent manoeuvring their way in silent proximity to the other, putting on coffee, making a sandwich, reaching around the other for the cutlery drawer ...

She was damned if she was going to suffer through a third.

So she selected her mother's favourite coffee shop in town. Getting her there would take little effort – nothing more than a text message saying she could really go for another mother-daughter chat, and would she like to meet up, say ten-ish. She knew there was a chance Erin might not feel up to the prospect of another heart-to-heart, but Avery was fairly certain she would accept the invitation nonetheless, if for no other reason than equating it to some sort of dutiful penance. Not that the thought pleased her. Rather it made her want to grab her mum, and either remind her of – or condemn her for – all the platitudes by which she had raised her daughter. All the be-your-own-person lectures. All the self-actualization books and articles asserting femininity, so often dog-eared and left on her bedside table. (*You can have it all. Don't defer your dreams and goals for anyone. No means no. Stay strong. Accept no limitations on your aspirations.*) She wanted to shake her until it revived the very beliefs Erin had seemingly only ever championed for her daughter. And if that revival resulted in her mother having to move on, then, for Christ's sake, move on. Because if there was any lasting shame to be felt, more than the infidelity (assuming there had even been any literal occasion of that sin to forgive, which

Avery seriously doubted), it was her mother's disassociation from all that she had once preached. The denial of her own will. The slow and insidious subversion of her belief in happiness.

As for her dad ...

Well, Avery's father had always been the silent tinkerer, had he not? That was just who he was. Stuffed away in the garage, or his studio room, intent on this plug-in application for that audio output, or this new condenser mic to be used with that new second-hand digital soundboard, plucked for a steal on Kijiji. But as immersed as he could get, from time to time he still needed an outlet for his passion. For so long, she had been that person. Over the years she had learned most all of his sound-engineering terms by rote without ever really understanding what they actually were and what they actually did. But that was okay. She knew he had to bounce that enthusiasm off someone ... someone who mattered to him. And that someone was not her mother. For as long as Avery could recall, that someone had never been her mother.

That said, getting her dad to venture from his recording lair on a weekend morning proved surprisingly easy even though the convention of coffee shops had never been a part of his routine. But then again, the stakes were incredibly high. After all, in his mind the suspicion of a wandering spouse had come out of nowhere. His up was suddenly down, his black, white. What had been a well-ordered life a few short weeks before was now nothing less than a nightmare from which nothing ... not his sound console, nor his folk club duties, nor his music chat rooms could save him. All it had taken was a phone call telling him to meet both of them at Erin's regular coffee shop. (And then a responding call on his part to clarify whether Erin went to the Coffee Break up in the strip mall next to the pharmacy, or the little independent café downtown around the corner from the post office that he couldn't remember the name of.)

“Aves, what the hell are you up to?”

Avery reached out and grabbed Erin’s sleeve to hold her there. “Oh look ... it’s Dad,” she said, with her eyes locked on her phone, but her grip still firmly on her mother. Ross sat down with an amplified measure of silence, even for him – the moral superiority he felt in the matter at hand giving him no cause to shy away from their public meeting place. “Nice of you to find the time, Rinn. What with all those hours at that new part-time job.”

“Dad!”

He leaned back, threw his palms up. “Hey, she’s the one with some guy–”

“You don’t know that.”

“Actually I do, Aves.” He leaned towards his wife. “Turns out you were seen. Spotted right out in the open, in the middle of the day. Jesus, Erin, you really think you could drive one town over and be anonymous. Or did you just not give a shit–” He turned to his daughter, tapped the table with his forefinger. “Bill had a service call on the shore road. Saw her and some other woman cruising the beach. A bunch of college dudes chatting them up out by the breakwater. Christ, and everybody has the nerve to call my home studio a mid-life crisis. Quite the sight you must have been, Erin ... doing your cougar routine.”

“Dad, come on.”

“ So ... tell me, is it one guy. Or are you doing the bunch of them?”

Erin glared at Ross, then turned to her daughter. “This should be fun,” she said and pushed herself out from the table. “I’ll get us coffee.”

“Nope, I will,” her daughter replied, sliding her phone into her hip pocket.

Ross folded his arms and stared out the window, his voice quivering. "Actually, I don't think I can do this after all, kiddo. Not if she's going to sit there like nothing happened."

"Maybe nothing did happen! Or at least nothing as bad as you're imagining."

"Bill saw her!"

"Jesus, Dad–"

"Aves, I'm sorry. You mean well, but you're in over your head here."

Erin, knowing how well that comment would go over, sat back in anticipation as her daughter dropped her sunglasses down her nose, put her hands on her hips and stared down at her dad.

"What?" he said, looking from one to the other.

Avery glanced about the café, chewing on the inside of her cheek, tapping her foot against a chair leg. Then, with eyes still averted, began. "A boy and his father are out riding their bikes. The son falls and breaks his leg. He needs surgery immediately."

"Aves, what are you doing? I taught you this one. The boy's mother–"

"THE BOY NEEDS SURGERY IMMEDIATELY," she cut in overtop of him. "But when they get to the hospital–"

"I know, I know. The boy is wheeled into emerg. The doctor says, 'I can't operate on this boy, he's my son'. Because the doctor is his mother, not his dad like everybody used to assume."

"Exactly," his daughter replied, then turned to glare and wait on her father. Ross threw his hands up in the air.

"No? Nothing?" She turned back to Erin. "Okay, you're up," she said, grabbing her sunglasses from the table and waving a hand back over her shoulder as she left.

"Avery!" He got up to follow, but then spun back towards Erin. "What the hell was that all about? For Christ's sake, I'm the one who taught her that riddle when–"

“Sit down, Ross,” Erin said and, when he made no immediate movement, added, “Please.”

Slowly he lowered himself back into the chair, peering at the top of her bowed head.

“She’s trying to break it to you gently.”

“Yeah, about you and this guy.”

“No, Ross. There really is no guy.” Only then did her gaze return, as she tried to complete the confession without the sting of the words. She studied his face, monitoring for any hint of epiphany. Upon its arrival Erin nodded slowly with a squint, bracing herself for the ensuing reaction.

“So ... the woman?” Ross mumbled into the space just above the napkins and sugar packets neatly arranged at the side of their table. “Well ... I doubt I can compete with that, can I?” he said finally, with a shrug and a sigh, his eyebrows up, the corners of his mouth turned down.

“Ross, it’s not about you–”

“Oh fuck off,” he burst out. “Do me a favour, okay? Don’t crap on the situation any more with some bullshit cliché. ‘It’s not about you.’ Christ, we’ve been married 23 years. It’s got everything to do with me.” He slapped the table, sending several of the packets airborne. “Fuck!”

She dropped her head again. “I’m sorry,” she whispered.

“Yeah, I’m sure you are.” He leaned an elbow on the table, as though getting ready to arm-wrestle, staring her down with a completely uncharacteristic lack of concern about any ripples of reaction from the rest of the coffee shop. She felt the weight of his gaze. The judging. She could not resist tethering his eyes to all the other sets she knew would be completely on his side, imagining the chorus of disapproving harmony – her mother, Leyla, the staff at her school, Audrey. Christ, Audrey would sign up to direct that choir. Then there were the more casual friends. The acquaintances.

The neighbours whom she never really got to know, passers-by from over the years, whom she could well imagine chipping in with a *well I never would have expected that of her*, once gossip of her dalliance spread its tentacles. Which it would. Creeping under doors and fences, into kitchen conversations and backyard barbecues. And it would stick to her like a stain. No matter how much time passed, and no matter how many fresher scandals would follow, that slight smell of disdain would always be there, hanging over her like a limp banner on a breezeless day.

"I'm just going to start talking," he began very slowly, eyes still trained on her. "And yes, I can hear you over there, saying to yourself, 'Well it's about time, Ross.' Like I'm the one who took everything for granted–"

"I'm not saying that."

"You're sure as hell thinking it."

"Goddamn it, Ross, don't tell me what I'm thinking," she said, putting up a finger, though he was absolutely spot on.

He raised his palms in mock surrender and after one very deliberate sigh, and a look about the room, began. "So ... this woman then." Erin nodded, this time returning the glare right back into his pupils. "I'm trying ... very hard ... not to say something catty ... or reactionary," he continued, his voice, she suddenly noticed, catching on the rough edges of his words. He shook his head, wiped his eyes. "That's not who I am. Surely to God, you know that much about me at least."

"Yes, I know that. Of course I know that." She reached out and held his forearm, and unlike the hands on his chest from a week before – just for a second – she felt life.

"I'm an open-minded person. I mean, Nadine at the arena office has been with Pam for years ... nobody cares. And I run a folk club for Christ's sake. Four or five same-sex couples on any given night, and Deirdre who did the rec department internship"

"Pre-op, yes," she said, finishing his thought. "I know."

They both sat a moment's silence, and at some point during the pause Erin realized she was caressing his arm. He too had taken notice, but did not pull away.

"So ... liking women. Is this ... a permanent thing?"

Erin glanced up at the ceiling, spending a few more precious seconds to consider her answer. "At this point, I think it's mostly a Meg thing."

"Meg," he repeated with a bit lip, and instantly she regretted using her name. "And is it ... love? I mean, should I assume this is not just some fling?"

"Honestly, I think it's probably a combination of the two," Erin replied, surprising herself both by her response and by the conviction of her tone. He too was caught off guard, so there was a delay before his reaction kicked in. He tried to yank his arm out from under her palm but she held on tight.

"Well, shit, Rinn, what exactly am I supposed to do with that information?"

"I know. I've put you in an awkward situation."

"Fuck, you think?"

She paused again to gather herself, swallowed hard and scrunched in closer to the table, before continuing in a whisper. "I think something like this was overdue, Ross." He opened his mouth to protest, but she continued overtop of him. "Whether it was me, or it was you, it was bound to happen. We were each other's first real option twenty-three years ago. Each other's first foray into sex. Each other's first love. But time has hammered that love down pretty thin, you have to admit... first to something more like friends, then ... well, just cohabitants. But we stayed all in, didn't we? Because it's safe and comfortable and reliable. And for years that was a good steady defence against–"

"Against what?"

She opened her mouth but faltered, seeing the tears soaking his eyes.

"Just say it, goddamn it. You don't love me."

"We don't love each other, Ross. Not anymore. Look at us. I'm stuck in my books and writing, when I'm not keeping myself occupied with extra-curriculars at school. You're always either at the folk club, or playing with your recording studio. We never talk. Maybe faintly cheer on each other's exploits, here and there, but if you're honest with yourself, you're probably way more content once I close the door behind you and leave you to your graphics and EQs, without my annoying comments about trees and fish ..."

"What?"

"You know, the graphic display on your laptop."

"What the hell are you talking about?"

"The sound waves on your recording computers. I used to joke how they looked like fish bones or trees reflected on a lake. Forget it. It's not important."

He was genuinely confused. "That wasn't annoying."

She sighed and dropped her fingers from his arm. "Well who the hell knew, Ross?"

There was more silence, interrupted only by a couple who came by, whose daughter Erin had taught a few years ago. They introduced themselves, told her how much their Hannah had liked that year ... especially the art classes and story time. Then another parent with more of the same, plus a bit of small talk about the weather and how the summer seemed to fly by so fast. Then back to silence.

"So what do we do?"

Erin shook her head.

"Well, it's clear you want to be with this woman, so–"

"What I want–" She stopped herself short, realizing to continue the thought would sound the epitome of selfishness and narcissism.

But something sour in his expression quickly bade her change her mind, and fuelled her on to speak her truth. "What I want ... what I need ... maybe it's both."

"Yeah? Think again, dear." He jumped up from the table, sending it skidding back over her lap, the pedestal below scraping up against her ankle. She lunged for him, both his arms this time, pulling him once again back down onto the chair.

"God, you're actually serious?"

"You know, I actually think I am," she snapped back, blurting it out in a manner that almost convinced him it was the first time she had considered the idea herself. "But first," she said, "to go back to what you were asking before. Like I was trying to say. I don't know if I'm now full-on attracted to women. But yes, it is a *woman* whom I have found myself liking. And it is a *woman* who had the answer to what was missing inside me." She took a long deep breath. "Ross, I'm going to look into getting my own apartment. Not in town, but renting something out at Pyette Beach maybe"

"For you and your *woman* to–"

"Damn it. For me, Ross ... me. To spend time writing. And reading. For my own version of a recording studio." Another pause. Another breath as she gazed down at the grip she had on his forearm. "That said ... I could still spend some time at the house, but only if that was something you wanted. Because for the most part, I'd be–"

"You'll be getting it on with your girlfriend."

"No, I actually have no clue whether there's any future with Meg. Given where things were left, I highly doubt it. But even if by some miracle it did come to pass …" She nodded her head by way of a concluding statement.

"Jesus, Rinn!" Ross finally pulled his arms free, folded them against his chest, shaking his head. "Why the hell should I sit here and agree to any of this?"

Her first thought was to inform him he had no choice. To remind him that he was not the author of her, that he had no powers to coerce her, so in the end his *signing-off* on whatever she decided was completely irrelevant. Her actual reply, however, took a different tack.

"You and I, we flat-lined a long time ago," she said.

He shook his head feverishly. "I don't agree–"

"Nevertheless, I am suggesting this arrangement because, despite it all, I don't know for certain if that flat line is the death-knell for the two of us. So in the meantime we could continue to be in each other's life like we were before."

He shook his head and seethed. "No. That's the thing, Rinn. It's not like we were before. It's fucking *nothing* like before."

Erin leaned in even closer, reached a hand up to his cheek and held it there, something she couldn't remember doing in a very long time.

"What will people say?" he whispered.

She closed her eyes and nodded again. "A lot. People always have lots to say. Trust me, Audrey will not be able to find the hours in the day. But it'll be against me mostly, not you ... if that's your concern. And besides, I wouldn't worry on that front too much. I've had my suspicions lately about the sort of people who wouldn't be able to resist chiming in with theories on what did us in. I suspect that's just what passes for sport amongst all the other flat-lined lives."

She found herself breathing slightly harder and brought a second hand up to frame his other cheek, leaned her forehead in against his.

"What about Avery?"

"Your daughter is stronger than the both of us put together."

She was outside herself. Watching a woman holding a scared

man's face. A man who for years had accelerated no pulse in her, whose cold hard chest only one week ago felt as lifeless and unresponsive as Leyla's father's had been, lying in his coffin. Her mother-in-law had spoken of a neighbour turning to the metaphysical when confronted with loss – resorting to straining her senses to connect with a spirit and a soul she could not locate, but could not bear to be without. Confronted with her own version of lifelessness, Erin had stumbled across the opposite response. She had found refuge *in* her senses. The tactile. The wind and sand and water, with all their caresses. And the caresses of one for whom the shoreline offered a similar haven. Absently her fingers stroked at his stubble.

"But, Ross, if I want to go back to the beach, I'm going to go back to the beach. And if I want to feel things, I'm going to feel things." She could sense his facial muscles tensing even as he leaned into her palms. "And if I should arouse the smile of someone else, or someone else arouses a smile from me, I'm going to feel nothing but good about it. I'm going to let that feeling wash over me. Like a wave." His eyes were closed. He was grimacing. But still she held him there. "Because that's who *we* were once upon a time, Ross. For a few brief moments in our steady little lives."

~5~

It was a dull and chilly November afternoon, in a grocery store of all places, when their paths finally crossed again. With her mind still occupied replaying the writers' session from an hour before (mostly replaying Barry's litany of asinine comments) Erin was scrolling through her phone in search of her shopping list when she barrelled into the opposing cart. Without looking up, she began the requisite apologies ... until she heard the opposing reply.

"Erin?"

She wore a pair of faded jeans along with a cropped leather coat. Her sunglasses rested up in her hair, which was tied back. She too had been distracted – by the insistent tug of a small flustered child. Seven, maybe eight Erin calculated. Also in tow was a shorter woman with a severe scowl, whose unfiltered voice warned the young boy of the consequences of his tantrum at a volume for all the store to hear. In her hands were two bags of potato chips that the woman fired over the boy and into Meg's cart. "None o' that's yours as long as you carry on," she decreed before turning her attention to a display of barbecue sauces nearby.

There was an irony to the fact the grocery store was not at Pyette Beach but in Erin's now-former home town, and that they would not have run into one another at all had Erin not been on one of her increasingly infrequent trips back to the house to grab some clothes and check the mail. Their odds of meeting should have been far more in favour of the lake, where Erin had made good on the promise to find a space of her own ... a studio apartment overtop of the local real estate office. Especially since she spent every evening and weekend walking down to the sand to let her boot tops nudge the lapping waves ... and to keep alive the possibility of finding Meg again. Keeping alive the possibility of apologizing. And making amends.

"Hi." Erin took a step forward around her cart, but stopped immediately upon examination of the expression that greeted her. Meg's eyes had shut – just for an instant. Nevertheless it was undeniably the look of someone preparing for discomfort. At that point the older woman broke in with a "Watch him!" and Meg spun to see the boy now completely inverted, feet in the air, face-first in the shopping trolley, as he stretched to examine a box of well-sugared cereal. "Terry, get out of there NOW," the woman screamed, as she grabbed him by the waist and hauled him over the handle.

Erin's eyes had stayed with Meg. The slackened spine, the hands squeezed into fists told her with uncategorical certainty that this was not a moment for seeking forgiveness. The realization hit with such obvious force that by the time Meg turned back and was readying herself with one long, slow preparatory breath Erin had already fled the scene, her cart of greens and proteins shoved aside and abandoned.

She sprinted for the exit, and into the parking lot, fumbling through her satchel for her keys, her eyesight blurred from the unstoppable onslaught of tears. She felt her voices rallying to incriminate her. Felt the shape of their words forming in her mouth. *You fucking idiot, you useless, selfish, pathetic little fucking idiot*, followed by inversions of the same sentiment that only grew stronger, and more audible as she continued to fail the task of unlocking her car. She smashed her hand against the window. Hurled her purse onto the pavement with enough force to send the contents spewing across the next parking space.

And then into that chaos, from behind, came a different voice altogether.

"Are you okay?"

She turned to find Meg, just a few feet away. Erin stepped closer to stare into the tint of Meg's sunglasses, searching back and forth into each eye for the faintest outline of expression, as she fought to see past the foreground of her own reflection.

"I'm so sorry," she watched herself say. "I just wanted to write something for you. I ... I just wanted to do something ..."

"Shhh." The response was accompanied by arms that surrounded her, and Erin sank into the embrace.

"I mean, in case we never got to see each other anymore ..." she continued mumbling, her cheek lodged against a shoulder.

Meg let go and pushed Erin out to arms length. "I'm not going to lie. I was pissed off," she said.

"I know."

"No, I mean really pissed off, Erin. That fucking hurt. Christ, you blindsided me. I went home and started throwing things around. Scared the shit out of my dog. So I ended up wandering around in the storm for most of the night."

"I know, I know. And I know you deserve an explanation, but for the life of me, I don't really have a good one. Except to say I never meant to expropriate your life–"

"But that's just it. None of that was me ... other than the name. Shit, who could live up to that amount of fiction? I just don't understand what you were hoping to accomplish."

Erin dodged eye contact, shaking her head rather violently. "I guess, I just ... lost my mind." She slapped her sides and gave a stomp of her heel, all by way of bearing down on the task of offering a more substantial response. "Look. I wanted you to let me in, alright? And when that wasn't happening, well, I guess I tried to pry you open on my own. So I could know you – or feel like I knew you – more than just this hot woman in a swimsuit."

Meg chuckled, lifted her friend's chin with one finger. "Hey, I think we both looked hot, okay?"

Erin managed a weak laugh, but then sighed. "Unfortunately, so did my husband's friend. He saw us."

Meg took a step backwards, crossed her arms. "So what happened?"

"We're on an indefinite break."

Meg shook her head and scoffed, and for a split second of weakness Erin's voices got through to wonder if this was the type of news that regularly followed this woman around.

"Because of me?"

"No. Not really. I'd say at most you were the catalyst to years of underlying conditions for separation."

A frown washed over Meg's face, contracting her forehead and squinting her eyes. "So in the end ... I was just a catalyst," she said, shaking her head and pawing at the pavement with a boot.

"No, I didn't mean *just*–"

"What, then? A hook-up? A fling? Mid-life crisis maybe?"

"No ... that's not what you were to *me*. You're making it all sound too shallow."

"Okay, your muse then," she pressed. "Seeing as you got so literary with my life."

"No. Come on–"

Meg began to pace. "Still not sounding legit enough, huh? How about some psycho-babble then. Lord knows I've sat through my share. Try this. In me, you were able to experience a truer version of yourself. I was the key to your self-actualization. The facilitator that awakened the dormant desires within your particular hierarchy of needs."

"Stop it."

"Too clinical?"

"Why are you doing this?"

"Because I'm a person, Erin! Not some need, or catalyst, or function of your life stage ... a person! Flesh and blood, and just as complicated and confusing as you." She was pacing in a tight circle, waving animated hands. "For Christ's sake, when do I just get to be that. An actual person with actual feelings for somebody ..." She orbited several more laps before realizing her words had trailed off inside her head. "And I can't get you out of my head," she said, coming to a halt and throwing her arms in the air. "Any suggestions how I might do that, Erin? I mean, I suppose I could write half a dozen short stories about what went wrong with your marriage."

"I deserve that."

"Damn straight you do," she said. "Let's see. Chapter One. Erin and ...?"

"Ross."

"Erin and Ross just came from two separate worlds. She was a debutante, the toast of Toronto's Rosedale, he was a dairy farmer from Bruce County."

"Off the mark a bit."

"Chapter Two. Money arguments. Ross drank his paycheque away while poor Erin was left with six hungry love-starved children."

"One daughter actually, and she's the apple of Ross's eye."

"Right. Okay ... Chapter Three. A marriage simply ran its course, and she met another?"

Erin looked up. "I might read that one," she replied.

For a moment they stood still and let the afternoon go about its business around them. Some kids were doing tricks on skateboards at the end of the parking lot. A mother hummed a tune as she wheeled a stroller past Erin's car. A pick-up truck revved its engine impatiently at a red light. Then Meg took a step back, looking up and down the length of the woman in front of her, made a joke about not being used to Erin wearing any clothes. She reached out her hand.

"Hi. My name's Megan Solomon. I'm thirty-seven years old. That lovable disaster you saw in there is my nephew Terry, and that was his mum, my stepsister Cecilia. She needs help from time to time – he's a lot. I run the candle shop at the corner of the Main Road and Lakeview Drive. I like to read science fiction. I have a weakness for country music that I'm not proud of. But most of all, I absolutely love the beach."

Erin looked down at the palm extending toward her, and reached out herself.

"It's very nice to meet you, Megan," she said.

~

The apartment has one chair and a daybed. There is a coffee table and one inset book shelf which she looks forward to filling gradually. There is a sink and a small two-burner stove next to a tiny counter beneath a small window that overlooks the side yard of the realtor's business. Beyond, in the distance, is the view of a quiet sand-bricked farmhouse, a throwback to when the town had not yet spread this far inland. It sits wisely in its age, settled and sunken into the landscape around it.

The far wall at the back of the apartment is dominated by a much larger window. It looks out beyond her writing desk, in the opposite direction of her beloved beach. She will often look up and take in the rolling length of the cornfield that stretches out beyond the town. She finds the vista an effective respite from the crowded chatter of ideas that can sometimes overwhelm her thoughts. On this windy late autumn morning she pauses to watch the remaining crop – now rusted and brittle – blowing in synchronized waves unimpeded all the way to the trees at the end of the farm. She finds a peace to this view – this lake of leaf and stalk – this finite horizon. It suggests comfort ... promises, faintly, a conclusion for her thoughts.

With her mind quieted, she unfolds her cherished clipping and once again reads the sparsely worded obituary, as she has done every morning since the day she happened upon it at the museum, while leafing through the summer's back issues of Pyette's weekly paper. Today she will work on her description of the balloon in particular. How it had shone against the sun when the woman proudly presented it, gripping the string tightly in the palm of her hand ... and when she had set it free, how the cloudless sky had swallowed it up, as it soared ever higher and higher over the sparkling waves.

And once she is satisfied – at least for the moment – with the depictions she has created and revised, Erin Leith will reward her efforts, with a long walk along a sandy shore.

Special Thanks

Once again I need to thank my tireless editor George Down for skillfully straightening out the bumps and rough edges of my writing in this latest book.

Thanks as well to the contributions, suggestions and insights from my other readers, Maggie Roberts VanHaften, AnnMarie Rowland, and foremost, Ande Ritchie. As I have stated before, nothing literary of mine leaves the house before first undergoing her consideration.

Thanks to Betty Ritchie for her unconditional support, to Bella Brough for her creative eye, to Alex Koster for being my beachside plot sounding board, to Mary Butchart for her stories about being the wife of a Great Lakes sailor, to Rich Spencer for making me aware of the joys and perils of storm chasing, to Kyra Brennan for inspiring me with her campaign to preserve sand dune habitat, to Sue Seguin for sharing descriptions of her family's life in Poland during and after WWII, and to Jacey and Brian Bedford for lending the creative space that is their Yorkshire home - where the original draft of this story first found its way out of my head.

Finally, thanks to Ande, Josh and Toby for their continual support as I entered into yet another literary venture. And to Ziggy (R.I.P.), Ginger and Otis for being the perfect footstools to see it through.

CPSIA information can be obtained
at www.ICGtesting.com
Printed in the USA
BVHW052135151022
649419BV00002B/7